UNWIN HY RIES

CW01017905

THA BE
THE DAY

INCLUDING
FOLLOW ON
ACTIVITIES

EDITED BY ROY BLATCHFORD

Unwin Hyman Short Stories
Openings   edited by Roy Blatchford
Round Two   edited by Roy Blatchford
School's OK   edited by Josie Karavasil and Roy Blatchford
Stepping Out   edited by Jane Leggett
That'll Be The Day   edited by Roy Blatchford
Sweet and Sour   edited by Gervase Phinn
It's Now or Never   edited by Jane Leggett and Roy Blatchford
Pigs is Pigs   edited by Trevor Millum
Dreams and Resolutions   edited by Roy Blatchford

Unwin Hyman Collections
Free As I Know   edited by Beverley Naidoo
Solid Ground   edited by Jane Leggett and Sue Libovitch
In Our Image   edited by Andrew Goodwyn

Unwin Hyman Plays
Stage Write   edited by Gervase Phinn

Published by
UNWIN HYMAN LIMITED
15/17 Broadwick Street
London W1V 1FP

Selection and notes © Roy Blatchford and Jane Leggett 1986
The copyright of each story remains the property of the author

Reprinted 1988

British Library Cataloguing in Publication Data

Unwin Hyman short stories for GCSE Vol. A
   1. Short stories, English   2. English fiction –
20th century
I. Blatchford, Roy
823'.01'08 [FS]   PR1309.S5

ISBN 0–7135–2711–0

Typeset by Typecast Limited, Tonbridge
Printed and bound in Great Britain by Billing & Sons Ltd. Worcester

Series cover design by Iain Lanyon
Cover illustration by Anne-Marie Blatchford © 1987

Contents

Introduction

Fiction has always been a major resource for teachers and students involved in the study of language and literature. Perhaps its most important contribution has been the enjoyment and pleasure that readers gain. Equally, fiction has been used because of its power to engage attention and the imagination, and give shape to personal experiences and expectations.

Many of the issues we wish to discuss with students are complex, challenging and probing. Reading fiction provides a chance to consider and reflect on them from a distance, before moving into the realm of personal experience and opinion. Fiction also offers a wealth of models of writing and expression that can be used to assist students in their own writing.

The aim of this collection is to provide a resource for students studying English and English Literature for the General Certificate of Secondary Education.

The stories have been selected first and foremost because they are fine examples of the short story genre, and are perhaps best enjoyed when read aloud and shared with a group of students. But they also offer opportunities to talk and write about issues that are of concern and relevance to young people.

Certain ideas and themes feature in more than one of the stories in 'That'll Be The Day': the power of memories, conflict between children and parents, relationships, individual freedom, political change. Opening the volume 'To Da-duh, In Memoriam' is a powerful tale of love and rivalry across the generations, themes echoed in Susan Hill's beautifully crafted 'The Custodian' and Graham Swift's arresting vignette 'Chemistry'.

'The Tunnel' takes the reader into the emotional lives of teenagers

4

breaking free of parental expectations, while 'An Affair of the Heart' offers moving insight into the adult looking back nostalgically to childhood. In turn, 'Lunch Hour Rush' highlights the common experience of tension between our private and public lives.

In contrast 'Memento Mori' and 'The Scoop' have been included as outstanding examples of comic writing, an ingredient frequently missing in anthologies for schools.

Especially written for this collection and previously unpublished is Beverley Naidoo's 'The Gun', a compelling and disturbing narrative revealing the horrors of apartheid in South Africa. The volume also includes personal essays by Beverley Naidoo and Graham Swift which serve to illuminate their own stories and the short story genre. Students will find these valuable both in their personal writing and in studying the genre.

The range of 'Follow On' activities is designed to present a variety of talking and writing assignments that will help students to gain in confidence and competence at using language effectively in any context. They also offer a range of approaches which will help students of all abilities, whether in building up a coursework folder or in preparing for essays written under examination conditions. More specifically, the activities aim to encourage students to:

▶ work independently and collaboratively

▶ consider:
  — the short story as a genre
  — language and style of a writer
  — structure and development of plot
  — development of character
  — setting

▶ examine the writer's viewpoint and intentions

▶ respond critically and imaginatively to the stories, orally and in writing

▶ read a variety of texts, including quite difficult ones

▶ read more widely.

One important footnote: the activities are divided under three broad headings — *Before*; *During*; *After Reading*. The intention is that students should engage with the text as closely as possible, from predicting storylines to analysing character's motivations. Teachers using the collection are therefore recommended to preview the 'Follow On' section before reading the stories with students.

Roy Blatchford

PAULE MARSHALL

To Da-duh, In Memoriam

This is the most autobiographical of the stories, a reminiscence largely of a visit I paid to my grandmother (whose nickname was Da-duh) on the island of Barbados when I was nine. Ours was a complex relationship — close, affectionate yet rivalrous. During the year I spent with her a subtle kind of power struggle went on between us. It was as if we both knew, at a level beyond words, that I had come into the world not only to love her and to continue her line but to take her very life in order that I might live.

Years later, when I got around to writing the story, I tried giving the contest I had sensed between us a wider meaning. I wanted the basic theme of youth and old age to suggest rivalries, dichotomies of a cultural and political nature, having to do with the relationship of western civilisation and the Third World.

Da-duh is an ancestor figure, symbolic for me of the long line of black women and men — African and New World — who made my being possible, and whose spirit I believe continues to animate my life and work. I wish to acknowledge and celebrate them. I am, in a word, an unabashed ancestor worshipper.

I did not see her at first I remember. For not only was it dark inside the crowded disembarkation shed in spite of the daylight flooding in from outside, but standing there waiting for her with my mother and sister I was still somewhat blinded from the sheen of tropical sunlight on the water of the bay which we had just crossed in the landing boat, leaving behind us the ship that had brought us from New York lying in the offing. Besides, being only nine years of age at the time and knowing nothing of islands I was busy attending to the alien sights and sounds of Barbados, the unfamiliar smells.

I did not see her, but I was alerted to her approach by my mother's hand which suddenly tightened around mine, and looking up I traced her gaze through the gloom in the shed until I finally made out the small, purposeful, painfully erect figure of the old woman headed our way.

Her face was drowned in the shadow of an ugly rolled-brim brown felt hat, but the details of her slight body and of the struggle taking place within it were clear enough — an intense, unrelenting struggle between her back which was beginning to bend ever so slightly under the weight of her eighty-odd years and the rest of her which sought to deny those years and hold that back straight, keep it in line. Moving swiftly toward us (so swiftly it seemed she did not intend stopping when she reached us but would sweep past us out the doorway which opened onto the sea and like Christ walk upon the water!), she was caught between the sunlight at her end of the building and the darkness inside — and for a moment she appeared to contain them both: the light in the long severe old-fashioned white dress she wore which brought the sense of a past that was still alive into our bustling present and in the snatch of white at her eye; the darkness in her black high-top shoes and in her face which was visible now that she was closer.

It was as stark and fleshless as a death mask, that face. The maggots might have already done their work, leaving only the framework of bone beneath the ruined skin and deep wells at the temple and jaw. But her eyes were alive, unnervingly so for one so old, with a sharp light that flicked out of the dim clouded depths like a lizard's tongue to snap up all in her view. Those eyes betrayed a child's curiosity about the world, and I wondered vaguely seeing them, and seeing the way the bodice of her ancient dress had collapsed in on her flat chest (what had happened to her breasts?), whether she might not be some kind of child at the same time that she was a woman, with fourteen children, my mother included, to prove it. Perhaps she was both, both child and woman, darkness and light, past and present, life and death — all the opposites contained and reconciled in her.

'My Da-duh,' my mother said formally and stepped forward. The name sounded like thunder fading softly in the distance.

'Child,' Da-duh said, and her tone, her quick scrutiny of my mother, the brief embrace in which they appeared to shy from each other rather than touch, wiped out the fifteen years my mother had been away and restored the old relationship. My mother, who was such a formidable figure in my eyes, had suddenly with a word been reduced to my status.

'Yes, God is good,' Da-duh said with a nod that was like a tic. 'He has spared me to see my child again.'

We were led forward then, apologetically because not only did Da-duh prefer boys but she also liked her grandchildren to be 'white,' that is, fair-skinned; and we had, I was to discover, a number of cousins, the outside children of white estate managers and the like, who qualified. We, though, were as black as she.

My sister being the oldest was presented first. 'This one takes after the father,' my mother said and waited to be reproved.

Frowning, Da-duh tilted my sister's face toward the light. But her frown soon gave way to a grudging smile, for my sister with her large mild eyes and little broad winged nose, with our father's high-cheeked Barbadian cast to her face, was pretty.

'She's goin' be lucky,' Da-duh said and patted her once on the cheek. 'Any girl child that takes after the father does be lucky.'

She turned then to me. But oddly enough she did not touch me. Instead, leaning close, she peered hard at me, and then quickly drew back. I thought I saw her hand start up as though to shield her eyes. It was almost as if she saw not only me, a thin truculent child who it was said took after no one but myself, but something in me which for some reason she found disturbing, even threatening. We looked silently at each other for a long time there in the noisy shed, our gaze locked. She was the first to look away.

'But Adry,' she said to my mother and her laugh was cracked, thin, apprehensive. 'Where did you get this one here with this fierce look?'

'We don't know where she came out of, my Da-duh,' my mother said, laughing also. Even I smiled to myself. After all I had won the encounter. Da-duh had recognised my small strength — and this was all I ever asked of the adults in my life then.

'Come, soul,' Da-duh said and took my hand. 'You must be one of those New York terrors you hear so much about.'

She led us, me at her side and my sister and mother behind, out of the shed into the sunlight that was like a bright driving summer rain and over to a group of people clustered beside a decrepit lorry. They were our relatives, most of them from St Andrews although Da-duh herself lived in St Thomas, the women wearing bright print dresses, the colours vivid against their darkness, the men rusty black suits that encased them like straight-jackets. Da-duh, holding fast to my hand, became my anchor as they circled round us like a nervous sea, exclaiming, touching us with their calloused hands, embracing us shyly. They laughed in awed bursts: 'But look Adry got big-big children!' / 'And see the nice things they wearing, wrist watch and all!' / 'I tell you, Adry has done all right for sheself in New York . . .'

Da-duh, ashamed at their wonder, embarrassed for them, admonished them the while. 'But oh Christ,' she said, 'why you all got to get on like you never saw people from "Away" before? You would think New York is the only place in the world to hear wunna. That's why I don't like to go anyplace with you St Andrews people, you know. You all ain't been colonised.'

We were in the back of the lorry finally, packed in among the barrels of ham, flour, cornmeal and rice and the trunks of clothes that my mother had brought as gifts. We made our way slowly through Bridgetown's clogged streets, part of a funereal procession of cars and open-sided buses, bicycles and donkey carts. The dim little limestone shops and offices along the way marched with us, at the same mournful pace, toward the same grave ceremony — as did the people, the women balancing huge baskets on top their heads as if they were no more than hats they wore to shade them from the sun. Looking over the edge of the lorry I watched as their feet slurred the dust. I listened, and their voices, raw and loud and dissonant in the heat, seemed to be grappling with each other high overhead.

Da-duh sat on a trunk in our midst, a monarch amid her

court. She still held my hand, but it was different now. I had
suddenly become her anchor, for I felt her fear of the lorry with
its asthmatic motor (a fear and distrust, I later learned, she held
of all machines) beating like a pulse in her rough palm.

As soon as we left Bridgetown behind though, she relaxed,
and while the others around us talked she gazed at the canes
standing tall on either side of the winding marl road. 'C'dear,'
she said softly to herself after a time. 'The canes this side are
pretty enough.'

They were too much for me. I thought of them as giant weeds
that had overrun the island, leaving scarcely any room for the
small tottering houses of sunbleached pine we passed or the
people, dark streaks as our lorry hurtled by. I suddenly feared
that we were journeying, unaware that we were, toward some
dangerous place where the canes, grown as high and thick as a
forest, would close in on us and run us through with their
stiletto blades. I longed then for the familiar: for the street in
Brooklyn where I lived, for my father who had refused to
accompany us ('Blowing out good money on foolishness,' he
had said of the trip), for a game of tag with my friends under the
chestnut tree outside our ageing brownstone house.

'Yes, but wait till you see St Thomas canes,' Da-duh was
saying to me. 'They's canes father, bo,' she gave a proud
arrogant nod. 'Tomorrow, God willing, I goin' take you out in
the ground and show them to you.'

True to her word Da-duh took me with her the following day
out into the ground. It was a fairly large plot adjoining her
weathered board and shingle house and consisting of a small
orchard, a good-sized canepiece and behind the canes, where
the land sloped abruptly down, a gully. She had purchased it
with Panama money sent her by her eldest son, my uncle
Joseph, who had died working on the canal. We entered the
ground along a trail no wider than her body and as devious and
complex as her reasons for showing me her land. Da-duh strode
briskly ahead, her slight form filled out this morning by the
layers of sacking petticoats she wore under her working dress to
protect her against the damp. A fresh white cloth, elaborately
arranged around her head, added to her height, and lent her a
vain, almost roguish air.

Her pace slowed once we reached the orchard, and glancing

back at me occasionally over her shoulder, she pointed out the various trees.

'This here is a breadfruit,' she said. 'That one yonder is a papaw. Here's a guava. This is a mango. I know you don't have anything like these in New York. Here's a sugar apple.' (The fruit looked more like artichokes than apples to me.) 'This one bears limes . . .' She went on for some time, intoning the names of the trees as though they were those of her gods. Finally, turning to me, she said, 'I know you don't have anything this nice where you come from.' Then, as I hesitated: 'I said I know you don't have anything this nice where you come from . . .'

'No,' I said and my world did seem suddenly lacking.

Da-duh nodded and passed on. The orchard ended and we were on the narrow cart road that led through the canepiece, the canes clashing like swords above my cowering head. Again she turned and her thin muscular arms spread wide, her dim gaze embracing the small field of canes, she said — and her voice almost broke under the weight of her pride, 'Tell me, have you got anything like these in that place where you were born?'

'No.'

'I din' think so. I bet you don't even know that these canes here and the sugar you eat is one and the same thing. That they does throw the canes into some damn machine at the factory and squeeze out all the little life in them to make sugar for you all so in New York to eat. I bet you don't know that.'

'I've got two cavities and I'm not allowed to eat a lot of sugar.'

But Da-duh didn't hear me. She had turned with an inexplicably angry motion and was making her way rapidly out of the canes and down the slope at the edge of the field which led to the gully below. Following her apprehensively down the incline amid a stand of banana plants whose leaves flapped like elephants ears in the wind, I found myself in the middle of a small tropical wood — a place dense and damp and gloomy and tremulous with the fitful play of light and shadow as the leaves high above moved against the sun that was almost hidden from view. It was a violent place, the tangled foliage fighting each other for a chance at the sunlight, the branches of the trees locked in what seemed an immemorial struggle, one both necessary and inevitable. But despite the violence, it was pleasant, almost peaceful in the gully, and beneath the thick undergrowth the earth smelled like spring.

This time Da-duh didn't even bother to ask her usual question, but simply turned and waited for me to speak.

'No,' I said, my head bowed. 'We don't have anything like this in New York.'

'Ah,' she cried, her triumph complete. 'I din' think so. Why, I've heard that's a place where you can walk till you near drop and never see a tree.'

'We've got a chestnut tree in front of our house,' I said.

'Does it bear?' she waited. 'I ask you, does it bear?'

'Not anymore,' I muttered. 'It used to, but not anymore.'

She gave the nod that was like a nervous twitch. 'You see,' she said. 'Nothing can bear there.' Then, secure behind her scorn, she added, 'But tell me, what's this snow like that you hear so much about?'

Looking up, I studied her closely, sensing my chance, and then I told her, describing at length and with as much drama as I could summon not only what the snow in the city was like, but what it would be like here, in her perennial summer kingdom.

'. . . And you see all these trees you got here,' I said. 'Well, they'd be bare. No leaves, no fruit, nothing. They'd be covered in snow. You see your canes. They'd be buried under tons of snow. The snow would be higher than your head, higher than your house, and you wouldn't be able to come down into this here gully because it would be snowed under . . .'

She searched my face for the lie, still scornful but intrigued. 'What a thing, huh?' she said finally, whispering it softly to herself.

'And when it snows you couldn't dress like you are now,' I said. 'Oh no, you'd freeze to death. You'd have to wear a hat and gloves and galoshes and ear muffs so your ears wouldn't freeze and drop off, and a heavy coat. I've got a Shirley Temple coat with fur on the collar. I can dance. You wanna see?'

Before she could answer I began, with a dance called the Truck which was popular back then in the 1930s. My right forefinger waving, I trucked around the nearby trees and around Da-duh's awed and rigid form. After the Truck I did the Suzy-Q, my lean hips swishing, my sneakers sidling zigzag over the ground. 'I can sing,' I said and did so, starting with 'I'm Gonna

Sit Right Down and Write Myself a Letter,' then without pausing, 'Tea for Two,' and ending with 'I Found a Million Dollar Baby in a Five and Ten Cent Store.'

For long moments afterwards Da-duh stared at me as if I were a creature from Mars, an emissary from some world she did not know but which intrigued her and whose power she both felt and feared. Yet something about my performance must have pleased her, because bending down she slowly lifted her long skirt and then, one by one, the layers of petticoats until she came to a drawstring purse dangling at the end of a long strip of cloth tied round her waist. Opening the purse she handed me a penny. 'Here,' she said half-smiling against her will. 'Take this to buy yourself a sweet at the shop up the road. There's nothing to be done with you, soul.'

From then on, whenever I wasn't taken to visit relatives, I accompanied Da-duh out into the ground, and alone with her amid the canes or down in the gully I told her about New York. It always began with some slighting remark on her part: 'I know they don't have anything this nice where you come from,' or 'Tell me, I hear those foolish people in New York does do such and such . . .' But as I answered, recreating my towering world of steel and concrete and machines for her, building the city out of words, I would feel her give way. I came to know the signs of her surrender: the total stillness that would come over her little hard dry form, the probing gaze that like a surgeon's knife sought to cut through my skull to get at the images there, to see if I were lying; above all, her fear, a fear nameless and profound, the same one I had felt beating in the palm of her hand that day in the lorry.

Over the weeks I told her about refrigerators, radios, gas stoves, elevators, trolley cars, wringer washing machines, movies, airplanes, the cyclone at Coney Island, subways, toasters, electric lights: 'At night, see, all you have to do is flip this little switch on the wall and all the lights in the house go on. Just like that. Like magic. It's like turning on the sun at night.'

'But tell me,' she said to me once with a faint mocking smile, 'do the white people have all these things too or it's only the people looking like us?'

I laughed. 'What d'ya mean,' I said. 'The white people have even better.' Then: 'I beat up a white girl in my class last term.'

'Beating up white people!' Her tone was incredulous.

'How do you mean!' I said, using an expression of hers. 'She called me a name.'

For some reason Da-duh could not quite get over this and repeated in the same hushed, shocked voice, 'Beating up white people now! Oh, the lord, the world's changing up so I can scarce recognise it anymore.'

One morning toward the end of our stay, Da-duh led me into a part of the gully that we had never visited before, an area darker and more thickly overgrown than the rest, almost impenetrable. There in a small clearing amid the dense bush, she stopped before an incredibly tall royal palm which rose cleanly out of the ground, and drawing the eye up with it, soared high above the trees around it into the sky. It appeared to be touching the blue dome of sky, to be flaunting its dark crown of fronds right in the blinding white face of the late morning sun.

Da-duh watched me a long time before she spoke, and then she said very quietly, 'All right, now, tell me if you've got anything this tall in that place you're from.'

I almost wished, seeing her face, that I could have said no.

'Yes,' I said. 'We've got buildings hundreds of times this tall in New York. There's one called the Empire State Building that's the tallest in the world. My class visited it last year and I went all the way to the top. It's got over a hundred floors. I can't describe how tall it is. Wait a minute. What's the name of that hill I went to visit the other day, where they have the police station?'

You mean Bissex?'

'Yes, Bissex. Well, the Empire State Building is way taller than that.'

'You're lying now!' she shouted, trembling with rage. Her hand lifted to strike me.

'No, I'm not,' I said. 'It really is, if you don't believe me I'll send you a picture postcard of it soon as I get back home so you can see for yourself. But it's way taller than Bissex.'

All the fight went out of her at that. The hand poised to strike me fell limp to her side, and as she stared at me, seeing not me but the building that was taller than the highest hill she knew, the small stubborn light in her eyes (it was the same amber as the flame in the kerosene lamp she lit at dusk) began to fail. Finally, with a vague gesture that even in the midst of her defeat still tried to dismiss me and my world, she turned and started back through the gully, walking slowly, her steps groping and uncertain, as if she were suddenly no longer sure of the way, while I followed triumphant yet strangely saddened behind.

The next morning I found her dressed for our morning walk but stretched out on the Berbice chair in the tiny drawing room where she sometimes napped during the afternoon heat, her face turned to the window beside her. She appeared thinner and suddenly indescribably old.

'My Da-duh,' I said.

'Yes, nuh,' she said. Her voice was listless and the face she slowly turned my way was, now that I think back on it, like a Benin mask, the features drawn and almost distorted by an ancient abstract sorrow.

'Don't you feel well?' I asked.

'Girl, I don't know.'

'My Da-duh, I goin' boil you some bush tea,' my aunt, Da-duh's youngest child, who lived with her, called from the shed roof kitchen.

'Who tell you I need bush tea?' she cried, her voice assuming for a moment its old authority. 'You can't even rest nowadays without some malicious person looking for you to be dead. Come girl,' she motioned me to a place beside her on the old-fashioned lounge chair, 'give us a tune.'

I sang for her until breakfast at eleven, all my brash irreverent Tin Pan Alley songs, and then just before noon we went out into the ground. But it was a short, dispirited walk. Da-duh didn't even notice that the mangoes were beginning to ripen and would have to be picked before the village boys got to them. And when she paused occasionally and looked out across the canes or up at her trees it wasn't as if she were seeing them but something else. Some huge, monolithic shape had imposed itself, it seemed, between her and the land, obstructing her vision. Returning to the house she slept the entire afternoon on the Berbice chair.

She remained like this until we left, languishing away the mornings on the chair at the window gazing out at the land as if it were already doomed; then, at noon, taking the brief stroll with me through the ground during which she seldom spoke, and afterwards returning home to sleep till almost dusk sometimes.

On the day of our departure she put on the austere, ankle length white dress, the black shoes and brown felt hat (her town clothes she called them), but she did not go with us to town. She saw us off on the road outside her house and in the midst of my mother's tearful protracted farewell, she leaned down and whispered in my ear, 'Girl, you're not to forget now to send me the picture of that building, you hear.'

By the time I mailed her the large coloured picture postcard of the Empire State Building she was dead. She died during the famous '37 strike which began shortly after we left. On the day of her death England sent planes flying low over the island in a show of force — so low, according to my aunt's letter, that the downdraft from them shook the ripened mangoes from the trees in Da-duh's orchard. Frightened, everyone in the village fled into the canes. Except Da-duh. She remained in the house at the window so my aunt said, watching as the planes came swooping and screaming like monstrous birds down over the village, over her house, rattling her trees and flattening the young canes in her field. It must have seemed to her lying there that they did not intend pulling out of their dive, but like the hardback beetles which hurled themselves with suicidal force against the walls of the house at night, those menacing silver shapes would hurl themselves in an ecstasy of self-immolation onto the land, destroying it utterly.

When the planes finally left and the villagers returned they found her dead on the Berbice chair at the window.

She died and I lived, but always, to this day even, within the shadow of her death. For a brief period after I was grown I went to live alone, like one doing penance, in a loft above a noisy factory in downtown New York and there painted seas of sugar-cane and huge swirling Van Gogh suns and palm trees striding like brightly-plumed Tutsi warriors across a tropical landscape, while the thunderous tread of the machines downstairs jarred the floor beneath my easel, mocking my efforts.

GRAHAM SWIFT

Chemistry

The pond in our park was circular, exposed, perhaps fifty yards across. When the wind blew, little waves travelled across it and slapped the paved edges, like a miniature sea. We would go there, Mother, Grandfather and I, to sail the motor-launch Grandfather and I made out of plywood, balsawood and varnished paper. We would go even in the winter — especially in the winter, because then we would have the pond to ourselves — when the leaves on the two willows turned yellow and dropped and the water froze your hands. Mother would sit on a wooden bench set back from the perimeter; I would prepare the boat for launching. Grandfather, in his black coat and grey scarf, would walk to the far side to receive it. For some reason it was always Grandfather, never I, who went to the far side. When he reached his station I would hear his 'Ready!' across the water. A puff of vapour would rise from his lips like the smoke from a muffled pistol. And I would release the launch. It worked by a battery. Its progress was laboured but its course steady. I would watch it head out to the middle while Mother watched behind me. As it moved it seemed that it followed an actual existing line between Grandfather, myself and Mother, as if Grandfather were pulling us toward him on some invisible cord, and that he had to do this to prove we were not beyond his reach. When the boat drew near him he would crouch on his haunches. His hands — which I knew were knotted, veiny and mottled from an accident in one of his chemical experiments — would reach out, grasp it and set it on its return.

The voyages were trouble-free. Grandfather improvised a wire grapnel on the end of a length of fishing line in case of shipwrecks or engine failure, but it was never used. Then one day — it must have been soon after Mother met Ralph — we watched the boat, on its first trip across the pond to Grandfather, suddenly become deeper, and deeper in the water. The motor cut. The launch wallowed, sank. Grandfather made several throws with his grapnel and pulled out clumps of green slime. I remember what he said to me, on this, the first loss in my life that I had witnessed. He said, very gravely: 'You must accept it — you can't get it back — it's the only way,' as if he were repeating something to himself. And I remember Mother's face as she got up from the bench to leave. It was very still and very white, as if she had seen something appalling.

It was some months after that Ralph, who was now a regular guest at weekends, shouted over the table to Grandfather: 'Why don't you leave her alone?!'

I remember it because that same Saturday Grandfather recalled the wreck of my boat, and Ralph said to me, as if pouncing on something: 'How about me buying you a new one? How would you like that?' And I said, just to see his face go crestfallen and blank, 'No!', several times, fiercely. Then as we ate supper Ralph suddenly barked, as Grandfather was talking to Mother: 'Why don't you leave her alone?!'

Grandfather looked at him. 'Leave her alone? What do you know about being left alone?' Then he glanced from Ralph to Mother. And Ralph didn't answer, but his face went tight and his hands clenched on his knife and fork.

And all this was because Grandfather had said to Mother: 'You don't make curry any more, the way you did for Alec, the way Vera taught you.'

It was Grandfather's house we lived in — with Ralph as an ever more permanent lodger. Grandfather and Grandmother had lived in it almost since the day of their marriage. My grandfather had worked for a firm which manufactured gold- and silver-plated articles. My grandmother died suddenly when I was only four; and all I know is that I must have had her looks. My mother said so and so did my father; and Grandfather, without saying anything, would often gaze curiously into my face.

At that time Mother, Father and I lived in a new house some distance from Grandfather's. Grandfather took his wife's death very badly. He needed the company of his daughter and my father; but he refused to leave the house in which my grandmother had lived, and my parents refused to leave theirs. There was bitterness all round, which I scarcely appreciated. Grandfather remained alone in his house, which he ceased to maintain, spending more and more time in his garden shed which he had fitted out for his hobbies of model making and amateur chemistry.

The situation was resolved in a dreadful way: by my own father's death.

He was required now and then to fly to Dublin or Cork in the light aeroplane belonging to the company he worked for, which imported Irish goods. One day, in unexceptional weather conditions, the aircraft disappeared without trace into the Irish Sea. In a state which resembled a kind of trance — as if some outside force were all the time directing her — my Mother sold up our house, put away the money for our joint future, and moved in with Grandfather.

My father's death was a far less remote event than my grandmother's, but no more explicable. I was only seven. Mother said, amidst her adult grief: 'He has gone to where Grandma's gone.' I wondered how Grandmother could be at the bottom of the Irish Sea, and at the same time what Father was doing there. I wanted to know when he would return. Perhaps I knew, even as I asked this, that he never would, that my childish assumptions were only a way of allaying my own grief. But if I really believed Father was gone for ever — I was wrong.

Perhaps too I was endowed with my father's looks no less than my grandmother's. Because when my mother looked at me she would often break into uncontrollable tears and she would clasp me for long periods without letting go, as if afraid I might turn to air.

I don't know if Grandfather took a secret, vengeful delight in my father's death, or if he was capable of it. But fate had made him and his daughter quits and reconciled them in mutual grief. Their situations were equivalent: she a widow and he a widower. And just as my mother could see in me a vestige of my father, so Grandfather could see in the two of us a vestige of my grandmother.

For about a year we lived quietly, calmly, even contentedly within the scope of this sad symmetry. We scarcely made any contact with the outside world. Grandfather still worked, though his retirement age had passed, and would not let Mother work. He kept Mother and me as he might have kept his own wife and son. Even when he did retire we lived quite comfortably on his pension, some savings and a widow's pension my mother got. Grandfather's health showed signs of weakening — he became rheumatic and sometimes short of breath — but he would still go out to the shed in the garden to conduct his chemical experiments, over which he hummed and chuckled gratefully to himself.

We forgot we were three generations. Grandfather bought Mother bracelets and ear-rings. Mother called me her 'little man'. We lived for each other — and for those two unfaded memories — and for a whole year, a whole harmonious year, we were really quite happy. Until that day in the park when my boat, setting out across the pond towards Grandfather, sank.

Sometimes when Grandfather provoked Ralph I thought Ralph would be quite capable of jumping to his feet, reaching across the table, seizing Grandfather by the throat and choking him. He was a big man, who ate heartily, and I was often afraid he might hit me. But Mother somehow kept him in check. Since Ralph's appearance she had grown neglectful of Grandfather. For example — as Grandfather had pointed out that evening — she would cook the things that Ralph liked (rich, thick stews, but not curry) and forget to produce the meals that Grandfather was fond of. But no matter how neglectful and even hurtful she might be to Grandfather herself, she wouldn't have forgiven someone else's hurting him. It would have been the end of her and Ralph. And no matter how much she might hurt Grandfather — to show her allegiance to Ralph — the truth was she really did want to stick by him. She still needed — she couldn't break free of it — this delicate equilibrium that she, he and I had constructed over the months.

I suppose the question was how far Ralph could tolerate not letting go with Grandfather so as to keep Mother, or how far Mother was prepared to turn against Grandfather so as not to lose Ralph. I remember keeping a sort of equation in my head: if Ralph hurts Grandfather it means I'm right — he doesn't really care about Mother at all; but if Mother is cruel to Grandfather (though she would only be cruel to him because she couldn't forsake him) it means she really loves Ralph.

But Ralph only went pale and rigid and stared at Grandfather without moving.

Grandfather picked at his stew. We had already finished ours. He deliberately ate slowly to provoke Ralph.

Then Ralph turned to Mother and said: 'For Christ's sake we're not waiting all night for him to finish!' Mother blinked and looked frightened. 'Get the pudding!'

You see, he liked his food.

Mother rose slowly and gathered our plates. She looked at me and said, 'Come and help'.

In the kitchen she put down the plates and leaned for several seconds, her back towards me, against the draining board. Then she turned. 'What am I going to do?' She gripped my shoulders. I remembered these were just the words she'd used once before, very soon after father's death, and then, too, her face had had the same quivery look of being about to spill over. She pulled me towards her. I had a feeling of being back in that old impregnable domain which Ralph had not yet penetrated. Through the window, half visible in the twilight, the evergreen shrubs which filled our garden were defying the onset of autumn. Only the cherry-laurel bushes were partly denuded — for some reason Grandfather had been picking their leaves. I didn't know what to do or say — I should have said something — but inside I was starting to form a plan.

Mother took her hands from me and straightened up. Her face was composed again. She took the apple-crumble from the oven. Burnt sugar and apple juice seethed for a moment on the edge of the dish. She handed me the bowl of custard. We strode, resolutely, back to the table. I thought: now we are going to face Ralph, now we are going to show our solidarity. Then she put down the crumble, began spooning out helpings and said to Grandfather, who was still tackling his stew: 'You're ruining our meal — do you want to take yours out to your shed?!'

Grandfather's shed was more than just a shed. Built of brick in one corner of the high walls surrounding the garden, it was large enough to accommodate a stove, a sink, an old armchair, as well as Grandfather's work-benches and apparatus, and to serve — as it was serving Grandfather more and more — as a miniature home.

I was always wary of entering it. It seemed to me, even before Ralph, even when Grandfather and I constructed the model launch, that it was somewhere where Grandfather went to be alone, undisturbed, to commune perhaps, in some obscure way, with my dead grandmother. But that evening I did not hesitate. I walked along the path by the ivy-clad garden wall. It seemed that his invitation, his loneliness were written in a form only I could read on the dark green door. And when I opened it he said: 'I thought you would come.'

I don't think Grandfather practised chemistry for any particular reason. He studied it from curiosity and for solace, as some people study the structure of cells under a microscope or watch the changing formation of clouds. In those weeks after Mother drove him out I learnt from Grandfather the fundamentals of chemistry.

I felt safe in his shed. The house where Ralph now lorded it, tucking into bigger and bigger meals, was a menacing place. The shed was another, a sealed-off world. It had a salty, mineral, unhuman smell. Grandfather's flasks, tubes and retort stands would be spread over his work-bench. His chemicals were acquired through connections in the metal-plating trade. The stove would be lit in the corner. Beside it would be his meal tray — for, to shame Mother, Grandfather had taken to eating his meals regularly in the shed. A single electric light bulb hung from a beam in the roof. A gas cylinder fed his bunsen. On one wall was a glass fronted cupboard in which he grew alum and copper sulphate crystals.

I would watch Grandfather's experiments. I would ask him to explain what he was doing and to name the contents of his various bottles.

And Grandfather wasn't the same person in his shed as he was in the house — sour and cantankerous. He was a weary, ailing man who winced now and then because of his rheumatism and spoke with quiet self-absorption.

'What are you making, Grandpa?'

'Not making — changing. Chemistry is the science of change. You don't make things in chemistry — you change them. Anything can change.'

He demonstrated the point by dissolving marble chips in nitric acid. I watched fascinated.

But he went on: 'Anything can change. Even gold can change.'

He poured a little of the nitric acid into a beaker, then took another jar of colourless liquid and added some of its contents to the nitric acid. He stirred the mixture with a glass rod and heated it gently. Some brown fumes came off.

'Hydrochloric acid and nitric acid. Neither would work by itself, but the mixture will.'

Lying on the bench was a pocket watch with a gold chain. I knew it had been given to Grandfather long ago by my grandmother. He unclipped the chain from the watch, then, leaning forward against the bench, he held it between two fingers over the beaker. The chain swung. He eyed me as if he were waiting for me to give some sign. Then he drew the chain away from the beaker.

'You'll have to take my word for it, eh?'

He picked up the watch and reattached it to the chain.

'My old job — gold plating. We used to take real gold and change it. Then we'd take something that wasn't gold at all and cover it with this changed gold so it looked as if it was all gold — but it wasn't.'

He smiled bitterly.

'What are we going to do?'

'Grandpa?'

'People change too, don't they?'

He came close to me. I was barely ten. I looked at him without speaking.

'Don't they?'

He stared fixedly into my eyes, the way I remembered him doing after Grandmother's death.

'They change. But the elements don't change. Do you know what an element is? Gold's an element. We turned it from one form into another, but we didn't make any gold — or lose any.'

Then I had a strange sensation. It seemed to me that Grandfather's face before me was only a cross section from some infinite stick of rock, from which, at the right point, Mother's face and mine might also be cut. I thought: every face is like this. I had a sudden giddying feeling that there is no end to anything. I wanted to be told simple, precise facts.

'What's that, Grandpa?'

'Hydrochloric acid.'

'And that?'

'Green vitriol.'

'And that?' I pointed to another unlabelled jar of clear liquid, which stood at the end of the bench, attached to a complex piece of apparatus.

'Laurel water. Prussic acid.' He smiled. 'Not for drinking.'

All that autumn was exceptionally cold. The evenings were chill and full of the rustlings of leaves. When I returned to the house from taking out Grandfather's meal tray (this had become my duty) I would observe Mother and Ralph in the living room through the open kitchen hatchway. They would drink a lot from the bottles of whisky and vodka which Ralph brought in and which at first Mother made a show of disapproving. The drink made Mother go soft and heavy and blurred and it made Ralph gain in authority. They would slump together on the sofa. One night I watched Ralph pull Mother towards him and hold her in his arms, his big lurching frame almost enveloping her, and Mother saw me, over Ralph's shoulder, watching from the hatchway. She looked trapped and helpless.

And that was the night that I got my chance — when I went to collect Grandfather's tray. When I entered the shed he was asleep in his chair, his plates, barely touched, on the tray at his feet. In his slumber — his hair dishevelled, mouth open — he looked like some torpid, captive animal that has lost even the will to eat. I had taken an empty spice jar from the kitchen. I took the glass bottle labelled HNO_3 and poured some of its contents, carefully, into the spice jar. Then I picked up Grandfather's tray, placed the spice jar beside the plates and carried the tray to the house.

I thought I would throw the acid in Ralph's face at breakfast. I didn't want to kill him. It would have been pointless to kill him — since death is a deceptive business. I wanted to spoil his face so Mother would no longer want him. I took the spice jar to my room and hid it in my bedside cupboard. In the morning I would smuggle it down in my trouser pocket. I would wait, pick my moment. Under the table I would remove the stopper. As Ralph gobbled down his eggs and fried bread . . .

I thought I would not be able to sleep. From my bedroom window I could see the dark square of the garden and the little patch of light cast from the window of Grandfather's shed. Often I could not sleep until I had seen that patch of light disappear and I knew that Grandfather had shuffled back to the house and slipped in, like a stray cat, at the back door.

But I must have slept that night, for I do not remember seeing Grandfather's light go out or hearing his steps on the garden path.

That night Father came to my bedroom. I knew it was him. His hair and clothes were wet, his lips were caked with salt; seaweed hung from his shoulders. He came and stood by my bed. Where he trod, pools of water formed on the carpet and slowly oozed outwards. For a long time he looked at me. Then he said: 'It was her. She made a hole in the bottom of the boat, not big enough to notice, so it would sink — so you and Grandfather would watch it sink. The boat sank — like my plane.' He gestured to his dripping clothes and encrusted lips. 'Don't you believe me?' He held out a hand to me but I was afraid to take it. 'Don't you believe me? Don't you believe me?' And as he repeated this he walked slowly backwards towards the door, as if something were pulling him, the pools of water at his feet drying instantly. And it was only when he had disappeared that I managed to speak and said: 'Yes. I believe you. I'll prove it.'

And then it was almost light and rain was dashing against the window as if the house were plunging under water and a strange, small voice was calling from the front of the house — but it wasn't Father's voice. I got up, walked out onto the landing and peered through the landing window. The voice was a voice on the radio inside an ambulance which was parked with its doors open by the pavement. The heavy rain and the tossing branches of a rowan tree obscured my view, but I saw the two men in uniform carrying out the stretcher with a blanket draped over it. Ralph was with them. He was wearing his dressing gown and pyjamas and slippers over bare feet, and he carried an umbrella. He fussed around the ambulance men like an overseer directing the loading of some vital piece of cargo. He called something to Mother who must have been standing below, out of sight at the front door. I ran back across the landing. I wanted to get the acid. But then Mother came up the stairs. She was wearing her dressing gown. She caught me in her arms. I smelt whisky. She said: 'Darling. Please, I'll explain. Darling, darling.'

But she never did explain. All her life since then, I think, she has been trying to explain, or to avoid explaining. She only said: 'Grandpa was old and ill, he wouldn't have lived much longer anyway.' And there was the official verdict: suicide by swallowing prussic acid. But all the other things that should have been explained — or confessed — she never did explain.

And she wore, beneath everything, this look of relief, as if she had recovered from an illness. Only a week after Grandfather's funeral she went into Grandfather's bedroom and flung wide the windows. It was a brilliant, crisp late-November day and the leaves on the rowan tree were all gold. And she said: 'There — isn't that lovely?'

The day of Grandfather's funeral had been such a day — hard, dazzling, spangled with early frost and gold leaves. We stood at the ceremony, Mother, Ralph and I, like a mock version of the trio — Grandfather, Mother and I — who had once stood at my father's memorial service. Mother did not cry.

She had not cried at all, even in the days before the funeral when the policemen and the officials from the coroner's court came, writing down their statements, apologising for their intrusion and asking their questions.

They did not address their questions to me. Mother said: 'He's only ten, what can he know?' Though there were a thousand things I wanted to tell them — about how Mother banished Grandfather, about how suicide can be murder and how things don't end — which made me feel that I was somehow under suspicion. I took the jar of acid from my bedroom, went to the park and threw it in the pond.

And then after the funeral, after the policemen and officials had gone, Mother and Ralph began to clear out the house and to remove the things from the shed. They tidied the overgrown parts of the garden and clipped back the trees. Ralph wore an old sweater which was far too small for him and I recognised it as one of Father's. And Mother said: 'We're going to move to a new house soon — Ralph's buying it.'

I had nowhere to go. I went down to the park and stood by the pond. Dead willow leaves floated on it. Beneath its surface was a bottle of acid and the wreck of my launch. But though things change they aren't destroyed. It was there, by the pond, when dusk was gathering and it was almost time for the park gates to be locked, as I looked to the centre where my launch sank, then up again to the far side, that I saw him. He was standing in his black overcoat and his grey scarf. The air was very cold and little waves were running across the water. He was smiling, and I knew: the launch was still travelling over to him, unstoppable, unsinkable, along that invisible line. And his hands, his acid-marked hands, would reach out to receive it.

SUSAN HILL

The Custodian

At five minutes to three he climbed up the ladder into the loft. He went cautiously, he was always cautious now, moving his limbs warily, and never going out in bad weather without enough warm clothes. For the truth was that he had not expected to survive this winter, he was old, he had been ill for one week, and then the fear had come over him again, that he was going to die. He did not care for his own part, but what would become of the boy? It was only the boy he worried about now, only he who mattered. Therefore, he was careful with himself, for he had lived out this bad winter, it was March, he could look forward to the spring and summer, could cease to worry for a little longer. All the same he had to be careful not to have accidents, though he was steady enough on his feet. He was seventy-one. He knew how easy it would be, for example, to miss his footing on the narrow ladder, to break a limb and lie there, while all the time the child waited, panic welling up inside him, left last at the school. And when the fear of his own dying did not grip him, he was haunted by ideas of some long illness, or incapacitation, and if he had to be taken into hospital, what would happen to the child, then? *What would happen?*

But now it was almost three o'clock, almost time for him to leave the house, his favourite part of the day, now he climbed on hands and knees into the dim, cool loft and felt about among the apples, holding this one and that one up to the beam of light coming through the slats in the roof, wanting the fruit he finally chose to be perfect, ripe and smooth.

The loft smelled sweetly of the apples and pears laid up there since the previous autumn. Above his head, he heard the scrabbling noises of the birds, house martins nesting in the eaves, his heart lurched with joy at the fresh realisation that it was almost April, almost spring.

He went carefully down the ladder, holding the chosen apple. It took him twenty minutes to walk to the school but he liked to arrive early, to have the pleasure of watching and waiting, outside the gates.

The sky was brittle blue and the sun shone, but it was very cold, the air still smelled of winter. Until a fortnight ago there had been snow, he and the boy had trudged back and forwards every morning and afternoon over the frost-hard paths which led across the marshes, and the stream running alongside of them had been iced over, the reeds were stiff and white as blades.

It had thawed very gradually. Today, the air smelled thin and sharp in his nostrils. Nothing moved. As he climbed the grass bank onto the higher path, he looked across the great stretch of river, and it gleamed like a flat metal plate under the winter sun, still as the sky. Everything was pale, white and silver, a gull came over slowly and its belly and the undersides of its wings were pebbly grey. There were no sounds here except the sudden chatter of dunlin swooping and dropping quickly down, and the tread of his own feet on the path, the brush of his legs against grass clumps.

He had not expected to live this winter.

In his hand, he felt the apple, hard and soothing to the touch, for the boy must have fruit, fruit every day, he saw to that, as well as milk and eggs which they fetched from Maldrun at the farm, a mile away. His limbs should grow, he should be perfect.

Maldrun's cattle were out on their green island in the middle of the marshes, surrounded by the moat of steely water, he led them across a narrow path like a causeway, from the farm. They were like toy animals, or those in a picture seen from this distance away, they stood motionless, cut-out shapes of black and white. Every so often, the boy was still afraid of going past the island of cows, he gripped the old man's hand and a tight expression came over his face.

'They can't get at you, don't you see? They don't cross water, not cows. They're not bothered about you.'

'I know.'

And he did know — and was still afraid. Though there had been days, recently, when he would go right up to the edge of the strip of water, and stare across at the animals, he would even accompany Maldrun to the half-door of the milking parlour, and climb up and look over, would smell the thick, sour, cow-smell, and hear the splash of dung on to the stone floor. Then, he was not afraid. The cows had great, bony haunches and vacant eyes.

'Touch one,' Maldrun had said. The boy had gone inside and put out a hand, though standing well back, stretched and touched the rough pelt, and the cow had twitched, feeling the lightness of his hand as if it were an irritation, the prick of a fly. He was afraid, but getting less so, of the cows. So many things were changing, he was growing, he was seven years old.

Occasionally, the old man woke in the night and sweated with fear that he might die before the boy was grown, and he prayed, then, to live ten more years, just ten, until the boy could look after himself. And some days it seemed possible, seemed, indeed, most likely, some days he felt very young, felt no age at all, his arms were strong and he could chop wood and lift buckets, he was light-headed with the sense of his own youth. He was no age. He was seventy-one. A tall bony man with thick white hair, and without any spread of spare flesh. When he bathed, he looked down and saw every rib, every joint of his own thin body, he bent an arm and watched the flicker of muscle beneath the skin.

As the path curved round, the sun caught the surface of the water on his right, so that it shimmered and dazzled his eyes for a moment, and then he heard the familiar, faint, high moan of the wind, as it blew off the estuary a mile or more away. The reeds rustled dryly together like sticks. He put up the collar of his coat. But he was happy, his own happiness sang inside his head, that he was here, walking along this path with the apple inside his hand inside his pocket, that he would wait and watch and then, that he would walk back this same way with the boy, that none of those things he dreaded would come about.

Looking back, he could still make out the shapes of the cows, and looking down, to where the water lay between the reed-banks, he saw a swan, its neck arched and its head below the surface of the dark, glistening stream, and it too was entirely still. He stopped for a moment, watching it, and hearing the thin sound of the wind and then, turning, saw the whole, pale stretch of marsh and water and sky, saw for miles, back to where the trees began, behind which was the cottage and then far ahead, to where the sand stretched out like a tongue into the mouth of the estuary.

He was amazed, that he could be alive and moving, small as an insect across this great, bright, cold space, amazed that he should count for as much as Maldrun's cows and the unmoving swan.

The wind was suddenly cold on his face. It was a quarter past three. He left the path, went towards the gate, and began to cross the rough, ploughed field which led to the lane, and then, on another mile to the village, the school.

Occasionally, he came here not only in the morning, and back again in the afternoon, but at other times when he was overcome with sudden anxiety and a desire to see the boy, to reassure himself that he was still there, was alive. Then, he put down whatever he might be doing and came, almost running, stumbled and caught his breath, until he reached the railings and the closed, black gate. If he waited there long enough, if it was dinner or break time, he saw them all come streaming and tumbling out of the green painted doors, and he watched desperately until he saw him, and he could loosen the grip of his hands on the railings, the thumping of his heart eased, inside his chest. Always, then, the boy would come straight down to him, running over the asphalt, and laughed and called and pressed himself up against the railings on the other side.

'Hello.'

'All right are you?'

'What have you brought me? Have you got something?'

Though he knew there would be nothing, did not expect it, knew that there was only ever the fruit at home-time, apple, pear or sometimes, in the summer, cherries or a peach.

'I was just passing through the village.'

'Were you doing the shopping?'

'Yes. I only came up to see . . .'

'We've done reading. We had tapioca for pudding.'

'That's good for you. You should eat that. Always eat your dinner.'

'Is it home-time yet?'

'Not yet.'

'You will be here won't you? You won't forget to come back?'

'Have I ever?'

Then, he made himself straighten his coat, or shift the string shopping bag over from one hand to the other, he said, 'You go back now then, go on to the others, you play with them,' for he knew that this was right, he should not keep the child standing here, should not show him up in front of the rest. It was only for himself that he had come, he was eaten up with his own concern, and fear.

'You go back to your friends now.'

'You will be here? You will be here?'

'I'll be here.'

He turned away, they both turned, for they were separate, they should have their own ways, their own lives. He turned and walked off down the lane out of sight of the playground, not allowing himself to look back, perhaps he went and bought something from the shop, and he was calm again, no longer anxious, he walked back home slowly.

He did not mind all the walking, not even in the worst weather. He did not mind anything at all in this life he had chosen, and which was all-absorbing, the details of which were so important. He no longer thought anything of the past. Somewhere, he had read that an old man has only his memories, and he had wondered at that, for he had none, or rather, they did not concern him, they were like old letters which he had not troubled to keep. He had, simply, the present, the cottage, and the land around it, and the boy to look after. And he had to stay well, stay alive, he must not die yet. That was all.

But he did not often allow himself to go up to the school like that, at unnecessary times, he would force himself to stay and sweat out his anxiety and the need to reassure himself about the child, in some physical job, he would beat mats and plant vegetables in the garden, prune or pick from the fruit trees or walk over to see Maldrun at the farm, buy a chicken, and wait until the time came so slowly around to three o'clock, and he could go, with every reason, could allow himself the pleasure of arriving there a little early, and waiting beside the gates, which were now open, for the boy to come out.

'What have I got today?'
   'You guess.'
   'That's easy. Pear.'
   'Wrong!' He opened his hand, revealing the apple.
   'Well, I like apples best.'
   'I know. I had a good look at those trees down the bottom this morning. There won't be so many this year. Mind, we've to wait for the blossom to be sure.'
   'Last year there were hundreds of apples. *Thousands*.' He took the old man's hand as they reached the bottom of the lane. For some reason he always waited until just here, by the white-beam tree, before doing so.
   'There were *millions* of apples!'
   'Get on!'
   'Well, a lot anyway.'
   'That's why there won't be so many this year. You don't get two crops like that in a row.'
   'Why?'
   'Trees wear themselves out, fruiting like that. They've to rest.'
   'Will we have a lot of pears instead then?'
   'I daresay. What have you done at school?'
   'Lots of things.'
   'Have you done your reading? That's what's the important thing. To keep up with your reading.'
He had started the boy off himself, bought alphabet and word picture books from the village, and, when they got beyond these, had made up his own, cut out pictures from magazines and written beside them in large clear letters on ruled sheets of paper. By the time the boy went to school, he had known more than any of the others, he was 'very forward', they had said, though looking him up and down at the same time for he was small for his age.
   It worried him that the boy was still small, he watched the others closely as they came out of the gates and they were all

taller, thicker in body and stronger of limb. His face was pale and curiously old looking beside theirs. He had always looked old.

The old man concerned himself even more, then, with the fresh eggs and cheese, milk and fruit, watched over the boy while he ate. But he did eat.

'We had meat and cabbage for dinner.'

Did you finish it?'

'I had a second helping. Then we had cake for pudding. Cake and custard. I don't like that.'

'You didn't leave it?'

'Oh no. I just don't like it, that's all.'

Now, as they came on to the marshes, the water and sky were even paler and the reeds beside the stream were bleached, like old wood left out for years in the sun. The wind was stronger, whipping at their legs from behind.

'There's the swan.'

'They've a nest somewhere about.'

'Have you seen it?'

'They don't let you see it. They go away from it if anybody walks by.'

'I drew a picture of a swan.'

'Today?'

'No. Once. It wasn't very good.'

'If a thing's not good you should do it again.'

'Why should I?'

'You'll get better then.'

'I won't get better at drawing.' He spoke very deliberately, as he so often did, knowing himself, and firm about the truth of things, so that the old man was silent, respecting it.

'He's sharp,' Maldrun's wife said. 'He's a clever one.'

But the old man would not have him spoiled, or too lightly praised.

'He's plenty to learn. He's only a child yet.'

'All the same, he'll do, won't he? He's sharp.'

But perhaps it was only the words he used, only the serious expression on his face, which came of so much reading and all that time spent alone with the old man. And if he was, as they said, so sharp, so forward, perhaps it would do him no good?

He worried about that, wanting the boy to find his place easily in the world, he tried hard not to shield him from things,

made him go to the farm to see Maldrun, and over Harper's fen
by himself, to play with the gamekeeper's boys, told him always
to mix with the others in the school playground, to do what
they did. Because he was most afraid, at times, of their very
contentment together, of the self-contained life they led, for in
truth they needed no one, each of them would be entirely happy
never to go far beyond this house: they spoke of all things, or of
nothing, the boy read and made careful lists of the names of
birds and moths, and built elaborate structures, houses and
castles and palaces out of old matchboxes, he helped with the
garden, had his own corner down beside the shed in which he
grew what he chose. It had been like this from the beginning,
from the day the old man had brought him here at nine months'
old and set him down on the floor and taught him to crawl, they
had fallen naturally into their life together. Nobody else had
wanted him. Nobody else would have taken such care.

Once, people had been suspicious, they had spoken to each
other in the village, had disapproved.

'He needs a woman there. It's not right. He needs someone
who knows,' Maldrun's wife had said. But now, even she had
accepted that it was not true, so that, before strangers, she
would have defended them more fiercely than anyone.

'He's a fine boy, that. He's all right. You look at him, look.
Well, you can't tell what works out for the best. You can never
tell.'

By the time they came across the track which led between the
gorse bushes and down through the fir trees, it was as cold as it
had been on any night in January, they brought in more wood
for the fire and had toast and the last of the damson jam and
mugs of hot milk.

'It's like winter. Only not so dark. I like it in winter.'

But it was the middle of March now, in the marshes the
herons and redshanks were nesting, and the larks spiralled up,
singing through the silence. It was almost spring.

So, they went on as they had always done, until the second of
April. Then, the day after their walk out to Derenow, the day
after they saw the kingfisher, it happened.

From the early morning, he had felt uneasy, though there was
no reason he could give for his fear, it simply lay, hard and cold
as a stone in his belly, and he was restless about the house from
the time he got up.

The weather had changed. It was warm and clammy, with low, dun-coloured clouds and, over the marshes, a thin mist. He felt the need to get out, to walk and walk, the cottage was dark and oddly quiet. When he went down between the fruit trees to the bottom of the garden the first of the buds were breaking into green but the grass was soaked with dew like a sweat, the heavy air smelled faintly rotten and sweet.

They set off in the early morning. The boy did not question, he was always happy to go anywhere at all but when he was asked to choose their route, he set off at once, a few paces ahead, on the path which forked away east, in the opposite direction from the village and leading, over almost three miles of empty marsh, towards the sea. They followed the bank of the river, and the water was sluggish, with fronds of dark green weed lying below the surface. The boy bent, and put his hand cautiously down, breaking the skin of the water, but when his fingers came up against the soft, fringed edges of the plants he pulled back.

'Slimey.'

'Yes. It's out of the current here. There's no freshness.'

'Will there be fish?'

'Maybe there will. Not so many.'

'I don't like it.' Though for some minutes he continued to peer between the reeds at the pebbles which were just visible on the bed of the stream. 'He asks questions,' they said. 'He takes an interest. It's his mind, isn't it — bright — you can see, alert, that's what. He's forever wanting to know.' Though there were times when he said nothing at all, his small, old-young face was crumpled in thought, there were times when he looked and listened with care and asked nothing.

'You could die here. You could drown in the water and never, never be found.'

'That's not a thing to think about. What do you worry over that for?'

'But you could, you could.'

They were walking in single file, the boy in front. From all the secret nests down in the reed beds, the birds made their own noises, chirring and whispering, or sending out sudden cries of warning and alarm. The high, sad call of a curlew came again and again, and then ceased abruptly. The boy whistled in imitation.

'Will it know it's me? Will it answer?'

He whistled again. They waited. Nothing. His face was shadowed with disappointment.

'You can't fool them, not birds.'

'You can make a blackbird answer you. You can easily.'

'Not the same.'

'Why isn't it?'

'Blackbirds are tame, blackbirds are garden birds.'

'Wouldn't a curlew come to the garden?'

'No.'

'Why wouldn't it?'

'It likes to be away from things. They keep to their own places.'

As they went on, the air around them seemed to close in further, it seemed harder to breathe, and they could not see clearly ahead to where the marshes and mist merged into the sky. Here and there, the stream led off into small, muddy pools and hollows, and the water in them was reddened by the rust seeping from some old can or metal crate thrown there and left for years, the stains which spread out looked like old blood. Gnats hovered in clusters over the water.

'Will we go onto the beach?'

'We could.'

'We might find something on the beach.'

Often, they searched among the pebbles for pieces of amber or jet, for old buckles and buttons and sea-smooth coins washed up by the tides, the boy had a collection of them in a cardboard box in his room.

They walked on, and then, out of the thick silence which was all around them came the creaking of wings, nearer and nearer and sounding like two thin boards of wood beaten slowly together. A swan, huge as an eagle, came over their heads, flying low, so that the boy looked up for a second in terror at the size and closeness of it, caught his breath. He said urgently, 'Swans go for people, swans can break your arm if they hit you, if they beat you with their wings. Can't they?'

'But they don't take any notice, so come on, you leave them be.'

'But they *can*, can't they?'

'Oh, they might.' He watched the great, grey-white shape go awkwardly away from them, in the direction of the sea.

A hundred yards further on, at the junction of two paths across the marsh, there was the ruin of a water mill, blackened after a fire years before, and half broken down, a sail torn off. Inside, under an arched doorway, it was dark and damp, the walls were coated with yellowish moss and water lay, brackish, in the mud hollows of the floor.

At high summer, on hot, shimmering blue days they had come across here on the way to the beach with a string bag full of food for their lunch, and then the water mill had seemed like a sanctuary, cool and silent, the boy had gone inside and stood there, had called softly and listened to the echo of his own voice as it rang lightly round and round the walls.

Now, he stopped dead in the path, some distance away.

'I don't want to go.'

'We're walking to the beach.'

'I don't want to go past that.'

'The mill?'

'There are rats.'

'No.'

'And flying things. Things that are black and hang upside down.'

'Bats? What's to be afraid of in bats? You've seen them, you've been in Maldrun's barn. They don't hurt.'

'I want to go back.'

'You don't have to go into the mill, who said you did? We're going on to where the sea is.'

'*I want to go back now.*'

He was not often frightened. But, standing there in the middle of the hushed stretch of fenland, the old man felt again disturbed himself, the fear that something would happen, here, where nothing moved and the birds lay hidden, only crying out their weird cries, where things lay under the unmoving water and the press of the air made him sweat down his back. Something would happen to them, something . . .

What could happen?

Then, not far ahead, they both saw him at the same moment, a man with a gun under his arm, tall and black and menacing as a crow against the dull horizon, and as they saw him, they also saw two mallard ducks rise in sudden panic from their nest in the reeds, and they heard the shots, three shots that cracked out and echoed for miles around, the air went on reverberating with the waves of terrible sound.

The ducks fell at once, hit in mid-flight so that they swerved, turned over, and plummeted down. The man with the shotgun started quickly forward and the grasses and reeds bent and stirred as a dog ran, burrowing to retrieve. 'I want to go back, *I want to go back.*'

Without a word, the old man took his hand, and they turned, walked quickly back the way they had come, as though afraid that they, too, would be followed and struck down, not caring that they were out of breath and sticky with sweat, but only wanting to get away, to reach the shelter of the lane and the trees, to make for home.

Nothing was ever said about it, or about the feeling they had both had walking across the marshes, the boy did not mention the man with the gun or the ducks which had been alive and in flight, then so suddenly dead. All that evening, the old man watched him, as he stuck pictures in a book, and tore up dock leaves to feed the rabbit, watched for signs of left-over fear. But he was only, perhaps, quieter than usual, his face more closed up, he was concerned with his own thoughts.

In the night, he woke, and got up, went to the boy and looked down through the darkness, for fear that he might have had bad dreams and woken, but there was only the sound of his breathing, he lay quite still, very long and straight in the bed.

He imagined the future, and his mind was filled with images of all the possible horrors to come, the things which would cause the boy shock and pain and misery, and from which he would not be able to save him, as he had been powerless today to protect him from the sight of the killing of two ducks. He was in despair. Only the next morning, he was eased, as it came back to him again, the knowledge that he had, after all, lived out the winter and ahead of them lay only light and warmth and greenness.

Nevertheless, he half-expected that something would still happen to them, to break into their peace. For more than a week, nothing did, his fears were quieted, and then the spring broke, the apple and pear blossom weighed down the branches in great, creamy clots, the grass in the orchard grew up as high as the boy's knees, and across the marshes the sun shone and shone, the water of the river was turquoise, and in the streams, as clear as glass, the wind blew warm and smelled faintly of salt and earth. Walking to and from the school every day, they saw more woodlarks than they had ever seen, quivering on the air high above their heads, and near the gorse bushes, the boy found a nest of leverets. In the apple loft, the house martins hatched out and along the lanes, dandelions and buttercups shone golden out of the grass.

It was on the Friday that Maldrun gave the boy one of the farm kittens, and he carried it home close to his body beneath his coat. It was black and white like Maldrun's cows. And it was the day after that, the end of the first week of spring, that Blaydon came, Gilbert Blaydon, the boy's father.

He was sitting outside the door watching a buzzard hover above the fir copse when he heard the footsteps. He thought it was Maldrun bringing over the eggs, or a chicken — Maldrun generally came one evening in the week, after the boy had gone to bed, they drank a glass of beer and talked for half an hour. He was an easy man, undemonstrative. They still called one another, formally, 'Mr Bowry,' 'Mr Maldrun.'

The buzzard roved backwards and forwards over its chosen patch of air, searching.

When the old man looked down again, he was there, standing in the path. He was carrying a canvas kitbag.

He knew, then, why he had been feeling uneasy, he had expected this, or something like it, to happen, though he had put the fears to the back of his mind with the coming of sunshine and the leaf-breaking. He felt no hostility as he looked at Blaydon, only extreme weariness, almost as though he were ill.

There was no question of who it was, yet above all he ought to have expected a feeling of complete disbelief, for if anyone had asked, he would have said that he would certainly never see the boy's father again. But now he was here, it did not seem surprising, it seemed, indeed, somehow inevitable. Things had to alter, things could never go on. Happiness did not go on.

'Will you be stopping?'

Blaydon walked slowly forward, hesitated, and then set the kitbag down at his feet. He looked much older.

'I don't know if it'd be convenient.'

'There's a room. There's always a room.'

The old man's head buzzed suddenly in confusion, he thought he should offer a drink or a chair, should see to a bed, should ask questions to which he did not want to know the answers, should say something about the boy. *The boy.*

'You've come to take him . . .'

Blaydon sat down on the other chair, beside the outdoors table. The boy looked like him, there was the same narrowness of forehead and chin, the same high-bridged nose. Only the mouth was different, though that might simply be because the boy's was still small and unformed.

'You've come to take him.'

'Where to?' He looked up. 'Where would I have, to take him to?'

But we don't want you here, the old man thought, we don't want anyone: and he felt the intrusion of this younger man, with the broad hands and long legs sprawled under the table, like a violent disturbance of the careful pattern of their lives, he was alien. *We don't want you.*

But what right had he to say that? He did not say it. He was standing up helplessly, not knowing what should come next, he felt the bewilderment as some kind of irritation inside his own head.

He felt old.

In the end, he managed to say, 'You'll not have eaten?'

Blaydon stared at him. 'Don't you want to know where I've come from?'

'No.'

'No.'

'I've made a stew. You'll be better for a plate of food.'

'Where is he?'

'Asleep in bed, where else would he be? I look after him, I know what I'm about. It's half-past eight, gone, isn't it? What would he be doing but asleep in his bed, at half-past eight?'

He heard his own voice rising and quickening, as he defended himself, defended both of them, he could prove it to this father or to anyone at all, how he'd looked after the boy. He would have said, what about you? Where have you been? What did you do for him? But he was too afraid, for he knew nothing about what rights Blaydon might have — even though he had never been near, never bothered.

'You could have been dead.'

'Did you think?'

'What was I to think? I knew nothing. Heard nothing.'

'No.'

Out of the corner of his eye, the old man saw the buzzard drop down suddenly, straight as a stone, on to some creature in the undergrowth of the copse. The sky was mulberry coloured and the honeysuckle smelled ingratiatingly sweet.

'I wasn't dead.'

The old man realised that Blaydon looked both tired and rather dirty, his nails were broken, he needed a shave and the wool at the neck of his blue sweater was unravelling. What was he to say to the boy then, when he had brought him up to be so clean and tidy and careful, had taken his clothes to be mended by a woman in the village, had always cut and washed his hair himself? What was he to tell him about this man?

'There's hot water. I'll get you linen, make you a bed. You'd best go up first, before I put out the stew. Have a wash.'

He went into the kitchen, took a mug and a bottle of beer and poured it out, and was calmed a little by the need to organise himself, by the simple physical activity.

When he took the beer out, Blaydon was still leaning back on the old chair. There were dark stains below his eyes.

'You'd best take it up with you.' The old man held out the beer.'

It was almost dark now. After a long time, Blaydon reached out, took the mug and drank, emptying it in four or five long swallows, and then, as though all his muscles were stiff, rose slowly, took up the kitbag, went towards the house.

When the old man had set the table and dished out the food, he was trembling. He tried to turn his mind away from the one thought. That Blaydon had come to take the boy away.

He called and when there was no reply, went up the stairs. Blaydon was stretched out on his belly on top of the unmade bed, heavy and motionless in sleep.

While he slept, the old man worried about the morning. It was Saturday, there would not be the diversion of going to school, the boy must wake and come downstairs and confront

Blaydon.

What he had originally said, was, your mother died, your father went away. And that was the truth. But he doubted if the boy so much as remembered; he had asked a question only once, and that more than two years ago.

They were content together, needing no one.

He sat on the straight-back chair in the darkness, surrounded by hidden greenery and the fumes of honeysuckle, and tried to imagine what he might say.

'This is your father. Other boys have fathers. This is your father who came back, who will stay with us here. For some time, or perhaps not for more than a few days. His name is Gilbert Blaydon.'

Will you call him 'father'?, will you . . .

'This is . . .'

His mind broke down before the sheer cliff confronting it and he simply sat on, hands uselessly in front of him on the outdoors table, he thought of nothing, and on white plates in the kitchen the stew cooled and congealed and the new kitten from Maldrun's farm slept, coiled on an old green jumper. The cat, the boy, the boy's father, all slept. From the copse, the throaty call of the night-jars.

'You'll be ready for breakfast. You didn't eat the meal last night.'

'I slept.'

'You'll be hungry.' He had his back to Blaydon. He was busy with the frying pan and plates over the stove. What had made him tired enough to sleep like that, from early evening until now, fully clothed on top of the bed! But he didn't want to know, would not ask questions.

The back door was open on to the path that led down between vegetable beds and the bean canes and currant bushes, towards the thicket. Blaydon went to the doorway.

'Two eggs, will you have?'

'If . . .'

'There's plenty.' He wanted to divert him, talk to him, he had to pave the way. The boy was there, somewhere at the bottom of the garden.

'We'd a hard winter.'

'Oh, yes?'

'Knee deep, all January, all February, we'd to dig ourselves out of the door. And then it froze — the fens froze right over, ice as thick as your fist. I've never known like it.'

But now it was spring, now outside there was the bright, glorious green of new grass, new leaves, now the sun shone.

He began to set out knives and forks on the kitchen table. It would have to come, he would have to call the boy in, to bring them together. What would he say? His heart squeezed and then pumped hard, suddenly, in the thin bone-cage of his chest.

Blaydon's clothes were creased and crumpled. And they were not clean. Had he washed himself? The old man tried to get a glimpse of his hands.

'I thought I'd get a job,' Blaydon said.

The old man watched him.

'I thought I'd look for work.'

'Here?'

'Around here. Is there work?'

'Maybe. I've not had reason to find out. Maybe.'

'If I'm staying on, I'll need to work.'

'Yes.'

'It'd be a help, I daresay?'

'You've a right to do as you think fit. You make up your own mind.'

'I'll pay my way.'

'You've no need to worry about the boy, if it's that. He's all right, he's provided for. You've no need to find money for him.'

'All the same . . '

After a minute, Blaydon walked over and sat down at the table.

The old man thought, he is young, young and strong and fit, he has come here to stay, he has every right, he's the father. He is . . .

But he did not want Blaydon in their lives, did not want the hands resting on the kitchen table, and the big feet beneath it.

He said, 'You could try at the farm. At Maldrun's. They've maybe got work there. You could try.'

'Maldrun's farm?'

'It'd be ordinary work. Labouring work.'

'I'm not choosy.'

The old man put out eggs and fried bread and bacon onto the plates, poured tea, filled the sugar basin. And then he had no more left to do, he had to call the boy.

But nothing happened as he had feared it, after all.

He came in. 'Wash your hands.' But he was already half way to the sink, he had been brought up so carefully, the order was not an order but a formula between them, regular, and of comfort.

'Wash your hands.'

'I've come to stay,' Blaydon said at once, 'for a bit. I got here last night.'

The boy hesitated in the middle of the kitchen, looked from one to the other of them, trying to assess this sudden change in the order of things.

'For a week or two,' the old man said. 'Eat your food.'

The boy got on to his chair. 'What's your name?'

'Gilbert Blaydon.'

'What have I to call you?'

'Either.'

'Gilbert, then.'

'What you like.'

After that, they got on with eating; the old man chewed his bread very slowly, filled, for the moment, with relief.

Maldrun took him on at the farm as a general labourer and then their lives formed a new pattern, with the full upsurge of spring. Blaydon got up, and ate his breakfast with them and then left, there was a quarter of an hour which the old man had alone with the boy before setting off across the marsh path to school, and in the afternoon, an even longer time. Blaydon did not return, sometimes, until after six.

At the weekend, he went off somewhere alone, but occasionally, he took the boy for walks; they saw the heron's nest, and then the cygnets, and once, a peregrine, flying over the estuary. The two of them were at ease together.

Alone, the old man tried to imagine what they might be saying to each other, he walked distractedly about the house, and almost wept, with anxiety and dread. They came down the path, and the boy was sitting up on Blaydon's shoulders, laughing and laughing.

'You've told him.'

Blaydon turned, surprised, and then sent the boy away. 'I've said nothing.'

The old man believed him. But there was still a fear for the future, the end of things.

The days lengthened. Easter went by, and the school holidays, during which the old man was happiest, because he had so much time with the boy to himself, and then it was May, in the early mornings there was a fine mist above the blossom trees.

'He's a good worker,' Maldrun said, coming over one evening with the eggs and finding the old man alone. 'I'm glad to have him.'

'Yes.'

'He takes a bit off your shoulders, I daresay.'

'He pays his way.'

'No. Work, I meant. Work and worries. All that.'

What did Maldrun know? But he only looked back at the old man, his face open and friendly, drank his bottled beer.

He thought about it, and realised that it was true. He had grown used to having Blaydon about, to carry the heavy things and lock up at night, to clear out the fruit loft and lop off the overhanging branches and brambles at the entrance to the thicket. He had slipped into their life, and established himself. When he thought of the future without Blaydon, it was to worry. For the summer was always short and then came the run down through autumn into winter again. Into snow and ice and cold, and the north-east wind scything across the marshes. He dreaded all that, now that he was old. Last winter, he had been ill once, and for only a short time. This winter he was a year older, anything might happen. He thought of the mornings when he would have to take the boy to school before it was even light, thought of the frailty of his own flesh, the brittleness of his bones, he looked in the mirror at his own weak and rheumy eyes.

He had begun to count on Blaydon's being here to ease things, to help with the coal and wood and the breaking of ice on pails, to be in some way an insurance against his own possible illness, possible death.

Though now, it was still only the beginning of summer, now, he watched Blaydon build a rabbit hutch for the boy, hammering nails and sawing wood, uncoiling wire skilfully. He heard them laugh suddenly together. This was what he needed, after all, not a woman about the place, but a man, the strength and ease of a man who was not old, did not fear, did not say 'Wash your hands', 'Drink up all your milk', 'Take care'.

The kitten grew, and spun about in quick, mad circles in the sun.

'He's a good worker,' Maldrun said.

After a while, the old man took to dozing in his chair outside, after supper, while Blaydon washed up, emptied the bins and then took out the shears, to clip the hedge or the grass borders, when the boy had gone to bed.

But everything that had to do with the boy, the business of rising and eating, going to school and returning, the routine of clothes and food and drink and bed, all that was still supervised by the old man. Blaydon did not interfere, scarcely seemed to notice what was done. His own part in the boy's life was quite different.

In June and early July, it was hotter than the old man could ever remember. The gnats droned in soft, grey clouds under the trees, and over the water of the marshes. The sun shone hard and bright and still the light played tricks so that the estuary seemed now very near, now very far away. Maldrun's cows tossed their heads, against the flies which gathered stickily in the runnels below their great eyes.

He began to rely more and more upon Blaydon as the summer reached its height, left more jobs for him to do, because he was willing and strong, and because the old man succumbed easily to the temptation to rest himself in the sun. He still did most of the cooking but he would let Blaydon go down to the shops and the boy often went with him. He was growing, his limbs were filling out and his skin was berry-brown. He lost the last of the pink-and-whiteness of babyhood. He had accepted Blaydon's presence without question and was entirely used to him, though he did not show any less affection for the old man, who continued to take care of him day by day. But he became less nervous and hesitant, more self-assured, he spoke of things in a casual, confident voice, learned much from his talks with Blaydon. He still did not know that this was his father. The old man thought there was no reason to tell him — not yet, not yet, they could go on as they were.

He was comforted by the warmth of the sun on his face, by the scent of the roses and the tobacco plants in the evening, the sight of the scarlet bean-flowers clambering higher and higher up their frame.

He had decided right at the beginning that he himself would ask no questions of Blaydon, would wait until he should be told. But he was not told. Blaydon's life might have begun only on the day he had arrived here. The old man wondered if he had been in prison, or else abroad, working on a ship, though he had no evidence for either. In the evenings they drank beer together and occasionally played a game of cards, though more often, Blaydon worked at something in the garden and the old man simply sat, watching him, hearing the last cries of the birds from the marshes.

With the money Blaydon brought in, they bought new clothes for the boy, and better cuts of meat, and then, one afternoon, a television set arrived with two men in a green van to erect the aerial.

'For the winter,' Blaydon said. 'Maybe you won't bother with it now. But it's company in the winter.'

'I've never felt the lack.'

'All the same.'

'I don't need entertainment. We make our own. Always have made our own.'

'You'll be glad of it once you've got the taste. I told you — it's for the winter.'

But the old man watched it sometimes very late in the evenings of August and discovered things of interest to him, new horizons were opened, new worlds.

'I'd not have known that,' he said. 'I've never travelled. Look at what I'd never have known.'

Blaydon nodded. He himself seemed little interested in the television set. He was mending the front fence, staking it all along with old wood given him by Maldrun at the farm. Now, the gate would fit closely and not swing and bang in the gales of winter.

It was on a Thursday night towards the end of August that Blaydon mentioned the visit to the seaside.

'He's never been,' he said, wiping the foam of beer from his top lip. 'He told me. I asked him. He's never been to the sea.'

'I've done all I can. There's never been the money. We've managed as best we could.'

'You're not being blamed.'

'I'd have taken him, I'd have seen to it in time. Sooner or later.'

'Yes.'

'Yes.'

'Well — I could take him.'

'To the sea?'

'To the coast, yes.'

'For a day? It's far enough.'

'A couple of days, I thought. For a weekend.'

The old man was silent. But it was true. The boy had never been anywhere and perhaps he suffered because of it, perhaps at school the others talked of where they had gone, what they had seen, shaming him; if that was so, he should be taken, should go everywhere, he must not miss anything, must not be left out.

'Just a couple of days. We'd leave first thing Saturday morning and come back Monday. I'd take a day off.'

He had been here three months now, and not missed a day off work.

'You do as you think best.'

'I'd not go without asking you.'

'It's only right. He's at the age for taking things in. He needs enjoyment.'

'Yes.'

'You go. It's only right.'

'I haven't told him, not yet.'

'You tell him.'

When he did, the boy's face opened out with pleasure, he licked his lips nervously over and over again in his excitement, already counting until it should be time to go. The old man went upstairs and sorted out clothes for him, washed them carefully and hung them on the line, he began himself to anticipate it all. This was right. The boy should go.

But he dreaded it. They had not been separated before. He could not imagine how it would be, to sleep alone in the cottage, and then he began to imagine all the possible accidents.

Blaydon had not asked him if he wanted to go with them. But he did not. He felt suddenly too tired to leave the house, too tired for any journeys or strangers, he wanted to sit on his chair in the sun and count the time until they should be back.

He had got used to the idea of Blaydon's continuing presence here, he no longer lived in dread of the coming winter. It seemed a long time since the days when he had been alone with the boy.

They set off very early on the Saturday morning, before the sun had broken through the thick mist that hung low over the marshes. Every sound was clear and separate as it came through the air, he heard their footsteps, the brush of their legs against the grasses long after they were out of sight. The boy had his own bag, bought new in the village, a canvas bag strapped across his shoulders. He had stood up very straight, eyes glistening, already his mind was filled with imaginary pictures of what he would see, what they would do.

The old man went back into the kitchen and put the kettle on again, refilled the teapot for himself and planned what he was going to do. He would work, he would clean out all the bedrooms of the house and sort the boy's clothes for any that needed mending; he would polish the knives and forks and wash the curtains and walk down to the village for groceries, he would bake a cake and pies, prepare a stew, ready for their return.

So that, on the first day, the Saturday, he scarcely had time to think of them, to notice their absence and in the evening, his legs and back ached, he sat for only a short time outside, after his meal, drunk with tiredness, and slept later than usual on the Sunday morning.

It was then that he felt the silence and emptiness of the house. He walked about it uselessly, he woke up the kitten and teased it with a feather so that it would play with him, distract his attention from his own solitude. When it slept again, he went out, and walked for miles across the still, hot marshes.

The water between the reed beds was very low and even dried up altogether in places, revealing the dark, greenish-brown slime below. The faint, dry whistling sound that usually came through the rushes was absent. He felt parched as the countryside after this long, long summer, the sweat ran down his bent back.

He had walked in order to tire himself out again but this

night he slept badly and woke out of clinging nightmares with a thudding heart, tossed from side to side, uncomfortable among the bedclothes. But tomorrow he could begin to count the strokes of the clock until their return.

He got up feeling as if he had never slept, his eyes were pouched and blurred. But he began the baking, the careful preparations to welcome them home. He scarcely stopped for food himself all day, though his head and his back ached, he moved stiffly about the kitchen.

When they had not returned by midnight on the Monday, he did not go down to the village, or across to Maldrun's farm to telephone the police and the hospitals. He did nothing. He knew.

But he sat up in the chair outside the back door all night with the silence pressing in on his ears. Once or twice his head nodded down on to his chest, he almost slept, but then jerked awake again, shifted a little, and sat on in the darkness.

He thought, they have not taken everything, some clothes are left, clothes and toys and books, they must mean to come back. But he knew that they did not. Other toys, other clothes, could be bought anywhere.

A week passed and the summer slid imperceptibly into autumn, like smooth cards shuffled together in a pack, the trees faded to yellow and crinkled at the edges.

He did not leave the house, and he ate almost nothing, only filled and refilled the teapot, and drank.

He did not blame Gilbert Blaydon, he blamed himself for having thought to keep the boy, having planned out their whole future. When the father had turned up, he should have known what he wanted at once, should have said, 'Take him away, take him now,' to save them this furtiveness, this deception. At night, though, he worried most about the effect it would have on the boy, who had been brought up so scrupulously, to be tidy and clean, to eat up his food, to learn. He wished there was an address to which he could write a list of details about the boy's everyday life, the routine he was used to following.

He waited for a letter. None came. The pear trees sagged under their weight of ripe, dark fruit and after a time it fell with soft thuds into the long grass. He did not gather it up and take it to store in the loft, he left it there for the sweet pulp to be burrowed by hornets and grubs. But sometimes he took a pear and ate it himself, for he had always disapproved of waste.

He kept the boy's room exactly as it should be. His clothes were laid out neatly in the drawers, his books lined on the single shelf, in case he should return. But he could not bother with the rest of the house, dirt began to linger in corners. Fluff accumulated greyly beneath beds. The damp patch on the bathroom wall was grown over with moss like a fungus when the first rain came in October.

Maldrun had twice been across from the farm and received no answer to his questions. In the village, the women talked. October went out in fog and drizzle, and the next time Maldrun came the old man did not open the door. Maldrun waited, peering through the windows between cupped hands, and in the end left the eggs on the back step.

The old man got up later and later each day, and went to bed earlier, to sleep between the frowsty, unwashed sheets. For a short while he turned on the television set in the evenings and sat staring at whatever was offered to him, but in the end he did not bother, only stayed in the kitchen while it grew dark around him. Outside, the last of the fruit fell onto the sodden garden and lay there untouched. Winter came.

*

In the small town flat, Blaydon set out plates, cut bread and opened tins, filled the saucepan with milk.

'Wash your hands,' he said. But the boy was already there, moving his hands over and over the pink soap, obediently, wondering what was for tea.

BEVERLEY NAIDOO

The Gun

For years it had been kept carefully secured on a rack above the bed, just beneath the thatch, inside 'Boss' Mackay's hut. The long, black barrel pointed towards a prize pair of spiralling kudu horns, fixed to the white-washed wall along with other trophies from the surrounding bush of Mackay's game-farm.

Esi had always been fascinated by the gun's silence and its power. Ever since an early memory of the great lifeless body of a leopard stretched out in the dusty yard — so much bigger than himself. Papa, his father, had been asked to tell the story many times. How during a terrible drought a male leopard had made its way between the huts early one morning, intent upon the enclosure for goats and chickens. Esi's father had managed to rouse Mackay who had grabbed his gun, firing a shot over the animal's head. But instead of bolting away, the creature had rushed at his attacker. The following shot brought the famished beast crashing, almost at Mackay's feet.

'Such is the desperation of hunger . . .' was how Papa would always end.

As a little boy, Esi had sat cross-legged on the leopard-skin mat gazing up at the gun, while his father cleaned and polished Mackay's room. A few years older, when his father's back was turned, he would stand by the bed, quickly stretching as tall as he could, to run his hand along the hard metal and smooth wood. He had longed to be taller, to let his hand explore the gun more fully. What would it feel like to let his finger curl gently around the strong metal of the trigger? Of course he had observed that the bolt and bullets were always removed, locked away separately in a drawer of the desk.

Now at fifteen, the rack within easy reach, he had been assigned the task of cleaning the room. But the gun was no longer above the bed. Ever since the police had come to warn about 'terrorists', Mackay had failed to follow the ritual of replacing the gun on its rack. Instead, he locked it in his cupboard.

The square shape and verandah of Mackay's hut (his 'bed-sitter in the bush' as he called it to his friends) distinguished it from the other round huts of the camp. It was mostly shut up for weeks at a time while he was away in Jo'burg, always taking the gun with him. A director of a large mining company, he lived in the city, only coming to his game-farm at intervals for a break.

'Too much work, too much noise!' he would say to Esi's father. Sometimes he came for a couple of days, sometimes more. No one knew when he would arrive . . . alone, with his grown-up daughter, or with friends; intending to watch the wild-life from the camouflaged hide-out at the water-hole, or to track and, when circumstance allowed, to shoot. Nowadays animals were only shot when necessary. As Mackay would tell visitors, his aim was preservation. Indeed wild-life flourished: impalas, zebras, wildebeests — to name but a few of the herds preyed on by lions, sometimes leopards, with their persistent hangers-on, the hyenas and jackals. Even elephants made their way across the territory from time to time.

It was simply by custom that it was called a 'farm', because apart from the small area in which a few crops were cultivated by Esi's family, it was entirely covered in age-old rough grass, stunted, tangled trees and bush. Close to the National Game Reserve and adjoining the Hendriks' game-farm, it could take you a day to walk across it from one end to the other.

Esi's father looked after the farm when Mackay was away, his main work being to stop poachers. As a child, Esi had found the constant dangers of following Papa through tall grass and rough bush thrilling and exciting. Poachers could be armed, while his father had only his short cutting-knife. But Papa could tell so much from noticing a broken twig, a flattened patch of grass, a piece of missing bark, vultures circling. If there was any trouble, he had to notify the white neighbour Hendriks, who would come with his gun and contact the police. Hendriks also made a point of coming over once a week to check all was in order.

However, even when Mackay was there, Esi noticed how his father was able to advise Mackay and answer his questions. Papa knew all about the movement and numbers of animals. If an animal was to be shot, it was Papa who quietly led the tracking to bring Mackay into the right position for shooting. It was always Papa who knew if poachers had set a trap, laying in turn one of his own. It was Papa who would shout the order for the poachers to put up their hands. While Mackay or Hendriks pointed the gun, it was Papa who would approach the trapped men to remove their belts, causing their trousers to fall to their ankles. It was Papa who would interpret for Mackay when the poachers spoke. Mackay depended almost totally on Papa. Indeed Esi had once overheard him saying as much to a visitor:

'You know I couldn't live in the city and run this place if it wasn't for my boss-boy Isaac.'

Yet Papa was never allowed to handle the gun.

Some forty kilometres from the farm was the village of Mapoteng, 'the place you get to in a round about way'. The land was poor and the people were poor. Even poorer since the white authorities had declared Mapoteng part of a 'homeland', to which black people had been sent in their thousands when their homes were not wanted close to the towns and cities of whites. Whole families had found themselves cleared off white-owned farms and 'black spots'; their homes bulldozed to the ground; themselves with their few possessions forced onto great grey government trucks, the 'GGs', and dumped in the dust of Mapoteng — to start life again. Here in this unknown place the government called their 'home', they found the earth hard and dry, cracked with over-use and drought. Here they found hunger. In desperation, some sought food in forbidden places.

It was when he was thirteen that Esi had been sent to stay with an aunt in Mapoteng, so he could attend the primary school. There he had begun to learn not only to read, but also what it was to eat only a few handfuls of 'pap' a day and little else. Although Papa would bring a large bag of mealie meal and some money for his sister, she was looking after another brother's family as well as her own. With ten hungry children in the house, food was often scarce.

In Mapoteng Esi found people who became silent on hearing who he was. They would look strangely at him, keeping their distance. He soon discovered that there were those who despised his father's job. In fact, it was stronger than that with some. It was hate. To them, his father was simply another detested policeman, protecting the white man's land and a source of food they sorely needed.

At first, Esi had been hurt and confused. Although he had said nothing, he wanted to defend Papa. However as his own stomach learnt to know the nagging ache of emptiness, he began to understand something of what people felt. Memories of the childish thrill and excitement of accompanying his father in the bush turned into an inner dread, fed by the troubled thought:

'If I had to live always in this place without food, I would also hunt.'

It was not the slow grip of hunger alone, however, that changed Esi . . .

From time to time news would somehow filter through to Mapoteng about an explosion, a protest, people shot by police. Most of this had seemed very far away to Esi, used to his small world around the camp. However, while others talked, he listened. There were men who lived apart from their families for most of the year, working deep down in the mines near the city. In hoarse voices (as if the dust had stuck in their throats) they spoke of meetings broken up by police with dogs, gas that burnt your eyes — and bullets. Some people had been moved from places where there had been boycotts and mass arrests, and where those who disappeared were sometimes rumoured to have escaped over the border to join the 'MKs'. Gradually he

The Gun   57

gathered that these MKs were people like themselves. But they
had resisted the trap of being pushed around and now lived
outside the white man's law, prepared to fight to be free of it —
even die, to overthrow it. It was plainly a dangerous matter, this
fighting for freedom.

Esi's familiar world was over-turned finally by the events on
one particular day. Without any warning, a line of army trucks
had come roaring, hurtling down, dust flying, through the rows
of mud and iron huts. Soldiers smashed open doors, wheeling
their guns and forcing people outside. The soldier who had
barged into his aunty's house had deftly swept her few treasured
pieces of crockery off the shelf with his rifle.

Horrified, shocked, they had been herded like cattle, to be
inspected by the white army chief. But most of the soldiers were
black, like themselves. Why were they doing this?

'Don't think you can hide anything from us! If you want to
help terrorists you know what you can expect!' the white officer
had grimly sneered, his words translated by the black soldier at
his side.

As Esi had watched these soldiers shoving and prodding their
young suspects with loaded guns, he had felt so angry — and so
helpless. They were all so helpless. If only *he* had a gun . . .

Shortly afterwards Esi had become very ill with a fever. Lack of
food had made him weak. When his father got word of this,
that was the end of schooling for Esi. Papa brought him home,
saying there was no point in going to school if it meant starving
first. Instead he would begin seriously teaching his son his own
work on the game-farm.

Esi remembered trying to talk to his father about what was
troubling him. But Papa had stopped him short, speaking
forcefully. He knew all about the raid on Mapoteng. Police had
also visited the farm to tell them about the 'terrorists' and how
they must report anything unusual. Papa had promised to do so.
Esi had to understand that he did his job as 'boss-boy' well so
that Mackay would depend on him. In return the family got
land, water, food. Indeed they were lucky. Couldn't Esi see how
foolish it was to question this? They might end up like the
people of Mapoteng, with nothing, and Esi would have to join

the queue for work on the mines.

Papa's voice softened.

'Listen Esi . . . This land was taken from our parents with guns. Those with guns can do what they please. You had better be very careful before you say "No" to a man with a gun. Can you stop a bullet with bare hands?'

Esi had shaken his head and kept quiet, his stomach knotted. He couldn't talk to his father and he had begun to dread the day when the poachers would be people he knew. How could he look them in the eye?

Now, some months later, Mackay was on one of his visits. Esi was performing his daily chore of collecting and chopping firewood, when Hendriks drove up in his truck. He seemed agitated, calling loudly to Esi:

'Waar's die baas?'

Almost before Esi put down the axe, Mackay appeared from his hut. Hendriks lowered his voice as he spoke, but Esi could still make out some words. Hendriks was saying something about 'terrorists' and an 'attack on a police-station' and 'no white man on the farm'. Then the two men went inside the hut for a drink.

When they came out again, Hendriks looked more relaxed and it seemed they had agreed on something. As they shook hands Hendriks said:

'Don't worry. He'll have your boss-boy and I'll give him a hand if he needs it. He'll soon get the hang of the place.'

'Well he just hasn't settled to anything since the army. Sometimes you wonder what happens to our boys in there. Those 'terrs' keep them tense, you know . . .' Mackay paused. 'Perhaps this is what he needs . . . sort himself out. I'll get him up here as soon as I can. Thanks for the warning!'

Mackay stood shading his eyes against the sun, watching Hendriks' truck manoeuvre through the narrow camp-gate and bump its way up along the dirt road. When the rumbling had faded away into the bush, Mackay called over to Esi.

'That's enough wood for now Esi . . . I won't need it tonight. Go and call your father. Tell him I'm leaving very soon.'

Papa didn't say anything until night-time when they were eating by the fire and Esi's mother raised the question.

'Why did he go like that?'

She had a way of saying 'he' which indicated that she was talking about Mackay.

'He's bringing someone . . .'

Papa paused and gave a wry, hoarse laugh.

'They want a white in charge . . . to stay. I think it's the one who is going to marry his daughter.'

Everyone was silent until Esi's mother clicked.

'That one's mouth is too big.'

Esi knew just what his mother meant. When the daughter's boyfriend had visited the farm once before, they were all relieved when he had left, even Papa who never showed his feelings much. At that time the young white man was doing his service in the army and had been on leave. But by now he must have finished his army service.

Esi was wondering whether to intervene in the conversation to report what Hendriks had said about 'terrorists', when Papa's cousin spoke. He had cycled over to Mapoteng during the day. Outside the shop he had heard people discussing news of a gun battle between three armed men and police at a place only a hundred kilometres south of Mapoteng. Apparently one man had been killed but two had got away. Some youngsters outside the shop had broken into song about MKs. Others, however, were worried there might be another house-to-house search in Mapoteng.

Early the following afternoon, there was the familiar sound of Mackay's landrover entering the camp. Esi saw immediately, however, that it was being driven by the young man Williams — and he was alone. When he jumped down from the driver's seat, he was carrying Mackay's gun. Although he could only be a few years older than Esi, there was something in his manner which reminded Esi of the sneering officer in the Mapoteng raid. His bush-green eyes narrowed on their target.

'What're you staring at? You've seen me before, haven't you? Go get your boss-boy for me. Be quick about it, jong!'

Esi could feel his face going hot, but he turned rapidly and sprinted off. Even Mackay never spoke to him like that, always calling him by his name.

Esi accompanied his father as he walked forward to greet the white man. He wanted to see how Papa would react.

'You remember me? . . . Boss Williams. Boss Mackay has asked me to come and look after his place, so we better get on, you and me. I don't want any trouble from the other boys either, O.K.?' He turned to Esi.

'You can get my bags out the back and carry them to my room.' Papa simply gave a slight nod. It was impossible to tell what he was thinking. His lined face remained quite impassive as father and son carried the young white man's cases.

Before long it was apparent that Williams assumed Esi to be his personal servant. Up till now Esi had taken instructions either from his father or Mackay, who had known him since he was little. But this man's manner was different. He didn't seem to care at all who Esi was, it was as if he was just a thing to be used.

Much of the time Williams would sit on the verandah outside Mackay's room, legs stretched out on a stool, a can of beer at his side, while cleaning or fiddling with Mackay's gun.

'Hey, come clean my boots!'

'You can wash the truck now!'

'Make my bed properly, jong! Don't just pull the sheets up like that!'

'Do you call these boots clean? If you were in the army I'd donder you! Do them again!'

'Go call the girl! I want her to do my washing this morning.'

At the last order, Esi had to fight to control himself. Who did this man think he was? Didn't he know that 'the girl' was Esi's own mother, old enough to be the white man's mother? When Esi found her, busy collecting wild spinach, his anger spilled out.

She tried to calm him. His temper would get him into trouble. He should try to be like his father.

'Papa just lets them push him around. I don't want to be like that!'

'Ha! What else can you do my young man?'

And with that his mother began walking slowly, steadily,

towards the camp to collect the dirty washing.

It was soon clear that Williams was a heavy drinker. He had brought his personal supply, Papa and Esi having unpacked half a dozen crates of beer and other drink from the landrover. On the first night, as Esi passed by in the dark he had looked into the lit-up sitting room and seen Mackay's special cabinet, usually kept locked, which was wide open with a half-full bottle of whisky on the table. Next morning there was an empty bottle in the bin.

Nor was it easy to get to sleep. The heavy silence of the bushveld night usually covered everything like a thick blanket of darkness, except for the customary night sounds — twitchings and chitterings, the odd screech or howl. But now that silence was shattered, with a radio blaring out music across the camp into the bush until after midnight.

When Hendriks arrived one afternoon, Williams invited him to have some beer.

'Hell man, I'm glad to see someone! How d'you live in this god-forsaken place? I must've been off my head to say "Yes" to the old man!'

The two men sat drinking and smoking on the verandah. Esi stayed out of sight, but within hearing. While he appeared to be polishing the black boots, he was listening intently for any news about the armed guerillas who had escaped. It seemed they still hadn't been captured and the search was being concentrated further south. Williams made out to Hendriks that he was patrolling the farm himself. It was a lie. He had only been down to the water-hole a couple of times, Mackay's gun slung from his shoulder. Esi and Papa had gone along with him, soon gathering that all Williams really wanted was to shoot a kudu bull, for a prize pair of horns like Mackay's. When Papa had mentioned that this wasn't the season for culling, for once Williams hadn't said anything. But Esi suspected that if a kudu came his way, he'd shoot.

Williams didn't only take over Esi's life. He began to give orders to Papa on the running of the farm. Papa kept quiet at first, fitting in the new instructions with what he normally did.

But the day after Hendrik's visit, when Williams ordered Papa to go to the shop at Mapoteng for cigarettes, Papa replied that he had planned to do a thorough tour of the farm that day. Something in his careful observations had made him uneasy. It would take him over two hours on the old bicycle just to get to Mapoteng. Perhaps the 'boss' would let one of the other workers go? However Esi heard Williams insist that it should be Papa.

'Don't you think I can manage here on my own?' he rasped.

Esi stopped sweeping the yard. He willed his father to answer back. Instead, his father, grim-faced but silent, slowly mounted the bicycle and rode off.

Esi began sweeping again. He jabbed the broom fiercely at the ground, causing the dust to scatter and fly, the anger he felt inside spilling out. How did Papa remain calm? Even before this man came, Papa had to play the same game with Mackay. 'Boss-boy'! 'Boy'! Yet if Mackay never came to the farm, Papa could still keep it running. Still, Mackay wasn't vicious like the man his daughter wanted to marry. What would happen if they did get married? Would Williams take over the farm? But whoever owned the place, Esi didn't want to be their policeman. Dust swirling up and around, he began to feel despair choking him.

'What the hell do you think you're doing? Can't you sweep properly? Hurry up with that job. I want you to come with me.'

With the gun slung at his side, and binoculars hanging around his neck, Williams set off through the bush, followed by Esi.

There were no animals at the water-hole. In the heat of the day, they would take to whatever shade they could find, coming for water only when the sun was going down. Williams thrust forward on his way to the other side of the water and began to follow a track through long dry grass and thorn trees up a low slope. With his father, Esi usually felt confident, Papa would move very quietly, always alert against possible danger. He could trust Papa's reactions despite his being unarmed.

Now, however, Esi felt nervous. Williams was too much on edge. At a sudden movement in the nearby bush, Esi froze. Williams whirled round, swinging the gun forward. But before he could locate his target, Esi had already looked into the wide eyes of a terrified little steenbuck, flickering past him through the tall grass. The gun was almost pointing at Esi before Williams lowered it, grunting a curse. This man was mad. Esi decided to lag as far behind him as possible.

As they moved further and further from the water-hole, Esi wondered whether Williams could find his way back. He was probably expecting to get his bearings from the top of the low hill since most of the land around was fairly flat.

Once at the top Williams walked to the edge of the ridge overlooking the other side. He scanned the veld below for a few minutes with his binoculars.

'Ja! There he is! What a beaut!'

Esi followed the direction of the binoculars. His eyes trailed along a dry river bed, searching the bush on its banks. Suddenly a slight movement defined the subtle curves of a grey kudu bull, its horns like converging branches. Lowering the binoculars, Williams signalled the way.

It was while they were still descending the ridge, that Esi noticed what looked like a cave. There was no time to investigate. However, he also observed that the grass seemed flattened in a patch around the cave. Looking back for a second or two, he steadied himself by lightly touching the branch of a tree. As he lifted his hand off the branch, careful to avoid the thorns, a piece of grey thread caught his eye. It was wool, as though a piece from someone's clothing had caught on the thorn. Whose was it? At that point Williams turned and whispered fiercely:

'Hurry up, jong! I'll donder you if you make me lose him.'

Esi's mind was now racing as he struggled to keep pace with Williams. Poachers wouldn't need a cave. They would come and go as quickly as possible, simply to set and collect from their traps. Their safety lay in merging back into Mapoteng. Maybe someone else had been hiding here. Esi could feel his heart pumping rapidly as he recalled the conversation on the verandah. The MKs still hadn't been captured. If he was Papa, he would contact Hendriks right away so the matter could be reported.

Williams turned around again.

'Come on, you . . .'

Before he could finish, he had tripped over an outstretched tree-root. A sharp, ear-splitting crack lashed the air, followed by a howl of pain. Williams' body lurched forward and struck the ground, the gun hurtling away on impact. When Esi reached him, he was squirming in the rough tall grass, clutching the leg he had shot.

'God, jong! . . . The safety catch came undone! . . . help me tie something around . . .'

Esi held back, watching as Williams struggled to tear off his shirt and tightly bandage his lower leg. The pain showed on his face.

'What're you waiting for? Help me up, jong!'

Still Esi hesitated, caught by an angry desire to laugh out loud at the helplessness of this man normally so high and mighty. Shot by his own gun — or Mackay's gun, what did it matter! When Esi did kneel down, Williams saw, perhaps for the first time, the contempt in the young man's eyes.

'You're strong enough to help me, damn it, aren't you?'

But as Williams began to put his weight on Esi in levering himself up, Esi suddenly let himself go limp . . .

No. He was not going to help this man.

Williams bellowed and swore, at Esi personally and 'the whole bloody lot of you'. The curses seemed to hang above them, echoing in the hot, otherwise silent bushveld air. Esi could see a dangerous look in Williams' eyes, as if the white man would have liked to crush him, injure him in some way too. He began to struggle to get away, but Williams was clutching him, forcing him down. With the white man's powerful hand edging towards his throat, Esi managed to free one leg, kick Williams on his wound, and wriggle free as a fearful scream rang in his ears.

Esi was shaking as he got to his feet. He saw the gun lying on the ground and almost without thinking picked it up and began to stumble back towards the ridge. His last image was of Williams trying to force himself up, groaning and cursing, with blood seeping through the make-shift bandage.

His mind was in turmoil. What had he done? He couldn't go back to the camp now. When it was found out what he had done, he would be arrested, surely beaten up and sentenced to years in jail. He'd heard plenty about jail in Mapoteng. In the white court all the sympathy would be for Williams. And if the man by any chance died . . .? Esi's mind blanked out. He didn't even know why he had taken the gun.

It had all happened so quickly. It seemed he had always been trapped and now he could quite easily be destroyed. Williams was like the soldiers who smashed up his aunty's house. He thought he had a right to push Esi around, while Esi had no right to disobey. Yes, Esi hated him and his power that ensnared all their lives. He didn't want to be like Papa, powerless, accepting the trap just so they could all keep on living — in the trap. Even maintaining the trap by catching poachers, black people like themselves, only starving. 'Such is the desperation of hunger' . . . He could hear Papa's own voice at the end of the leopard story. But how could you ever escape?

Esi came to the bottom of the ridge. He flopped down to rest against a boulder in a stony gulley, his head in his hands, Mackay's gun at his side. He must stop and think. He was going in the wrong direction, back towards the camp. Ah! He'd forgotten about the cave. What if those two MKs had been there, were there? Surely they were trying to escape the trap. They had arms. Arms against arms. At least they had a chance . . . So why shouldn't he have the gun? In Mapoteng he'd heard songs about young people going for 'training' outside the country. Somehow they found their way across the border. From here it was to the east. What was it like? The high barbed wire fence around the police station in Mapoteng? What about guards? Police and soldiers would surely be like flies on meat in the area near the border. He would have to travel by night . . .

Sitting alone in the gulley at the bottom of the ridge, Esi slowly realised that he had made his choice. He had made it at the moment he had let his body go limp, refusing to support Williams. There was no going back now. If only he could say good-bye to his family . . . hug them, especially his mother . . . for a last time try and explain to Papa. But it could not be. He would simply climb up to the cave . . . find out what was there . . . perhaps have a sleep . . . and at night, set out east, with the gun.

Personal Essay
by Beverley Naidoo

I recall that when I was at school in South Africa — at a school open only to white girls — the characters in many of the stories we read were animals. Most of our setbooks in Afrikaans (the main white language alongside English) were about whole families of them. These animals were given human feelings and there were sequels carrying on the saga of family history over generations.

The converse of this humanisation of animals in literature was that black characters in stories were frequently described in terms of animals. Probably the most famous of white South African animal stories is *Jock of the Bushveld* by Sir Percy FitzPatrick, first published in 1907. The book is largely devoted to the fiercely faithful character of the dog Jock, featuring the excitements of hunting and encountering wild-life in the bush of the Eastern Transvaal.

Most of the black people, however, are shadowy figures: 'natives' and 'boys' who do the carrying, set up the camps and cook the food. The exception is 'Jim', who is drawn larger than life through FitzPatrick's eyes, seen not only as Jock's 'ally and companion', but indeed as the dog's counterpart:
'His eyes glared like a wild beast's . . .
'He was simply a great, passionate, fighting savage.'

To understand fully the racist perspective of this 'classic' tale, it is relevant to know that FitzPatrick was a director of one of the most powerful mining companies that sprang up after the discovery of gold in the Transvaal. Indeed he played a leading role in encouraging the British government to go to war in South Africa against the white Afrikaners, at the turn of the century. The aim was to ensure that the golden wealth was channelled into British hands.

The raw gold had, of course, first to be channelled out of the earth by black hands. Millions of black men were to be forced, by a system of taxes and passes, to seek work below the earth in sub-human conditions as part of this process. Minimum expense, maximum profit. Millions of black families were to be broken. Millions of children were to see their fathers only once a year, at the end of their contracts. Millions of black people were to be arrested for offences under the 'pass' laws which controlled the flow of labour. FitzPatrick played a direct part in establishing all this, stating that only the 'civilised' were entitled to rights. No wonder the black characters in his book are portrayed as uncivilised and animal-like. No need to be concerned about sending 'savages' into a living hell.

It happens that the area in which I set 'The Gun' is also the Eastern Transvaal. I wasn't actually thinking of FitzPatrick at the time, but Mackay could essentially be a modern version in role and outlook. I chose the bushveld setting as it is the sort of countryside for which I developed very positive feelings as a child. We whites needed our illusions about our love of freedom, linked with open spaces and wild-life. Conservation having taken the place of hunting, Mackay would most certainly be a member of a Society for the Preservation of Wild-life, upholding ideas of freedom (for wild animals) and natural beauty.

As a child I also spent a number of holidays in the National Game Reserve. It was called the 'Kruger National Park' after the white Afrikaner leader who dominated many of the nineteenth century violent struggles for land against black communities. Unlike black South Africans, we whites could travel almost as freely as the animals through hundreds of miles of bush in this wild-life preservation area.

The place 'Mapoteng', on the borders of the game-farm, is of course both fictional — and real. Right across the vast landscape of South Africa there are places like it. The statistical picture is stark . . nearly four million people having had their homes destroyed, have been shunted across the rulers' chequer-board. For in this system — called 'apartheid' — if you are black and your labour is no longer wanted in a 'white' area, you can be trucked out of sight into some barren, arid waste where you are told to enjoy 'separate development'.

If we could fly over somewhere like Mapoteng, we would see to one side great expanses of sparsely inhabited, irrigated, mechanised white-owned farms producing beautiful crops and to the other side the magnificent bush of the game-farms. Squeezed in between, we would look down on thousands of small dwellings packed in the narrow 'black' zone . . . an area of semi-desert, eroded by forced over-crowding. A micro-map of land division throughout a country where life is governed by racist categories and laws.

I wrote 'The Gun' during the course of the State of Emergency called by the white rulers of South Africa in 1985/6. Faced with increasing black protest and resistance to apartheid policies, the authorities stepped up crude military force. The result? Increasing black protest and resistance. Esi is just one of many in a country on its way to revolution. The old order of 'white might and right' is being threatened as black South Africans, particularly the young, pit themselves against a most powerfully armed state.

The game-farm, with the dispossessed on its borders, is an embodi-ment for me of this society in which animals have been humanised — and people brutalised. I write merely as a witness, for it is the victims who see these contradictions most sharply and who believe there is only one path in the struggle to resolve them. The words of the poet Mongane Wally Serote say it simply, but deeply:

> 'we choose the weapons now
> either we live or we die
> how could we have existed for so long'

> *Song of Experience*

GRAHAM SWIFT

The Tunnel

All that spring and summer Clancy and I lived on the third floor of the old grey-brick tenement block in what might have been — we never really knew — Deptford or Bermondsey, Rotherhithe or New Cross. It was cheap because the block was due for demolition in the autumn and all the tenants had notice to quit by September. Most of them had gone already, so that those who remained were like survivors camping in a ruin. The vacated rooms were broken into at night and became the sources of foul smells. The old cream paintwork of the stair-wells, which here and there had darkened like enormous nicotine stains, was daubed with aerosol slogans and obscenities, and all through that hot drought of a summer the dust and litter from the streets, old pages of newspapers and polythene bags found their way up the flights of stairs, even as far as the third floor.

We didn't mind. It was all we could afford. We even relished the way we scooped out for ourselves a little haven, oblivious of the squalor around us. We were very young; we had only just left school. We were absorbed with each other, and we didn't think about what we'd do in a month's time, or two months', or when the winter came or we had to find somewhere else to live. We made love insatiably, the way very young people in love can. And when that summer arrived, endlessly sunny and hot, we thought of it as a blessing on ourselves, despite the dust and the smells, because it was possible to live quite well in that room, with its scant furniture, draughty windows and twin gas ring, so long as the weather was good. We even saved on the few clothes we had between us, because most of the time, with the dirty windows up and the hot air swimming in from the street, we wore nothing at all.

We had run away because that was the only way Clancy and I could go on seeing each other without Clancy's parents stopping us. We hadn't run far. Clancy's parents lived in a big, elegant Regency house by the park in Greenwich, and we knew that by going a couple of miles away, into the kind of area they preferred to think didn't exist, we'd be as safe as if we'd fled to the ends of the country. Clancy's father was a sort of financial expert who acted in an advisory capacity to the government and knew people in the House of Lords, and her mother came from good, sound pedigreed stock. They were not the kind of people to drag the police into a hunt for their daughter. But it was not beyond them to employ some private agency to track us down. And this was one of the reasons why, despite the scorching weather, we seldom left our third floor room, and when we did we kept a sharp eye open for men in slow-moving cars hugging the kerb, who might suddenly pull up, leap out and bundle Clancy inside.

Clancy's family was small. There were only Clancy herself, her mother and father and an ageing uncle who lived in seclusion in an old manor house in Suffolk where Clancy had spent summers when she was small. Clancy's father was obsessively proud of the fact that he was descended from a once noble line which could be traced back to the reign of Henry VIII; and — like Henry VIII himself — he had turned cold, as Clancy grew up, towards his wife and daughter because they were a perpetual reminder that he had no son. There was nothing, apparently, he could do to change this fact; but he was dead-set on preventing the only remaining eligible member of the family from being absorbed into the riff-raff.

I only met Clancy's mother and father once, and that was by accident one Saturday afternoon when Clancy had promised me her parents wouldn't be back till late. I had gone to the house in Greenwich. We made love on Clancy's bed, looked at her photo

albums and listened to the Beach Boys. We were sitting under
the vine in the conservatory and Clancy was urging me to
sample her Dad's stock of malt whisky, when her parents
suddenly turned up, having changed their plans for the evening.
Clancy's father asked me in icy, eloquent tones who the hell I
thought I was and told me to get out. It was as if my presence in
the house had no connection whatsoever with Clancy, as if I
were some random, alien intruder. He was a tall, poised, steel-
haired man with an air of having had the way of dealing with
such situations bred into him and of merely summoning it
automatically when required. I remember thinking that he and
Clancy's mother, and perhaps Clancy too, belonged to some
completely foreign world, a world that had ceased to exist long
ago or perhaps had only ever existed in people's minds; so that
whenever I thought of Clancy's parents, looking out from our
tenement window, I had to make an effort to believe they were
real.

My own parents were no obstacle to us. They had me late in
life so there was a big gap between our ages, which, oddly
enough, smoothed our relations. They did not care what I did
with my life. They had a council house in Woolwich and no
shining example to set me. I'd gone to a large comprehensive;
Clancy had gone to a classy girls' school in Blackheath; and we
might never have known each other if it wasn't for Eddy, a big,
hulking, raw-faced boy, who later joined the Royal Artillery,
who told me in his matter-of-fact way that he had robbed two
girls from Clancy's school of their virginity; and urged me to do
the same. With rather less swagger, I followed Eddy's bidding
('Tell them they'll thank you for it afterwards'), but, unlike
Eddy, I found the initial conquest wasn't an end in itself.

Clancy's parents soon found out — Clancy had a knack of
defiant truthfulness. I don't know what outraged them more:
the knowledge that their daughter was no longer intact and the
possible scandal of some schoolgirl pregnancy — or the mere
fact that Clancy associated with a boy from a council estate. I
knew what I would say to Clancy's father if I ever had to face
him. I would repeat to him something I'd read in the letters of
Gauguin (my favourite artist at that time and the only artist I
knew anything about). Gauguin says somewhere that the Tahi-

tians believed, unlike Europeans, that young people fall in love with each other because they have made love, not the other way round. I would explain that Clancy and I were good, regular Tahitians. But when the opportunity arose that Saturday afternoon — despite the sun shining through the vine leaves in the conservatory and Clancy's thin summer dress and the malt whisky in my head — Gauguin's South Sea paradise, which was only an image for what I felt for Clancy, paled before the cold aplomb of her father.

But Clancy's uncle did not share the parental disdain. This I discovered in about out third week in the tenement. Clancy had to go out now and then to draw money from her Post Office account, which was our sole source of income at that time. One day she returned with, of all things, a letter from her uncle. Apparently, she had written to him, explaining everything, confident of his trust, immediately after our flight, but for complete security had not given an address and had asked him to reply via a Post Office in New Cross. Clancy showed me the letter. It was written in a shaky hand and was full of fond platitudes and breezy assurances, with a certain wry relish about them, to the effect that Clancy had enough sense now to lead her own life.

I said: 'If he's so much on our side, why don't we go to him?' And I had a momentary vision, in Bermondsey, of dappled Constable landscapes.

'That's just where they'll look for us first.'

'But he won't tell them that you've got in touch.'

'No.'

And then Clancy explained about her uncle.

He had always had a soft spot for her and she for him, since the days when she used to play muddy, rebellious games round his estate in the summer. As she grew up (her uncle lost his wife and his health declined), it became clear that there were strong temperamental differences between him and her parents. He did not care for her father's sense of dignity or for his precious concern for the family name. He would be quite happy, he said, to sink heirless beneath the Suffolk soil. And he disapproved of the way Clancy was being rigorously groomed for some sort of outmoded high society.

'So you see,' said Clancy, putting away the letter, 'I had to tell him, didn't I? It's just what he'd want.'

She kissed the folded notepaper.

'And another thing,' — she got up, pausing deliberately before she went on. 'I know for a fact when Uncle dies I'll get everything; he won't leave a thing to Mum and Dad. So you see — we're all right.'

She said this with a kind of triumph. I realised it was an announcement she must have been saving up till the right moment, in order to make me glad. But I wasn't glad — though I put on a pleased expression. I'd never really reflected that this was what Clancy's background meant — the possibility of rich legacies, and I had never seen myself as a story-book adventurer who, having committed a daring elopement, would also gain a fortune. Nevertheless, it wasn't these things which disturbed me and (for the first time) cast a brief shadow over my life with Clancy. It was something else, something I couldn't understand. Clancy stood, smiling and pleased, at the window with the sun coming in behind her. She was wearing jeans and one of those tops made from gauzy, flimsy materials which she liked, I think, precisely because when she stood in front of the light you could see through them. It was the first fine weather of the spring, the first time we had been able to lift up our window wide to let some of the stinking air from inside out and some of the less stinking air from outside in. We'd been living together for three weeks, fugitives in a slum. The way happiness comes, I thought, is as important as the happiness itself.

From our tenement window you could see all that was ugly about that part of London. Directly opposite, across the road, was a junior school — high arched neo-Gothic windows, blackened brickwork, a pot-holed asphalt playground surrounded by a wall with wire netting on top — which, like the tenement, was due to be pulled down at the end of the summer. It stood at the edge of an area, to the left as we looked from the window, which had already been demolished or was in the process of being demolished. Everywhere there were contractors' hoardings, heaps of ruined masonry and grey corrugated metal fencing. Old blocks of terraced houses got turned into brick-coloured wildernesses over which dogs prowled and paths got trodden

where people took short cuts. To the right, on the other side of
the school, there was an odd, inexplicable patch of worn grass
with a stunted tree and a bench on it, and beyond that, on the
other side of a side street with a few tattered shops, was another
wasteland — of scrap yards, builders' yards, half defunct factories
and fenced-off sites which seemed to be depositories for cum-
bersome, utterly useless articles: heaps of car axles from which
the oil ran in black pools, stacks of rusted oil drums, even a pile
of abandoned shop-window dummies, their arms and legs sticking
up like some vision from Auschwitz. Beyond this was the
railway line to London Bridge on its brick arches, the tower
blocks, precincts and flimsy estates which had sprouted from
previous demolitions; while if you looked far round to the right
you could see the nodding antennae of cranes by the Thames.

All this we could survey at leisure, but because we were on
the third floor, when you lay on the bed (which we did most of
the time) and looked out of the window, you saw only the sky.
When the good weather came we lifted up the sash window
high and moved the bed according to the position of the
gradually shifting rectangle of sunshine, so that we could sunbathe
most of the day without ever going out. We turned nice and
brown and I told Clancy she was getting more and more like the
cinnamon-coloured South Sea girls Gauguin painted.

We would lie looking up at the blue sky. Now and then we'd
see flights of pigeons and gulls, or swallows swooping high up.
All day long we could hear the noise from the street, the
demolition sites and the breakers' yards, but after a while we
got accustomed to it and scarcely noticed it. We could tell time
was passing by the periods of commotion from the school
playground. We joked about our bed being a desert island, and
made up poems about ourselves and our room in the style of
John Donne.

I began to wish that when we'd hastily packed and fled I'd
brought more books with me. All I had was my life of Gauguin
and 'Sonnets, Lyrics and Madrigals of the English Renaissance'
which I'd borrowed from my English master at school and
never given back. I thought of my old English master, Mr Boyle,
a lot now. He had a passion for Elizabethan poetry which he
vainly tried to transmit to members of the fourth and fifth year,

who laughed at him, I amongst them, and spread rumours that
he was queer. Then in my last year, after I'd met Clancy, I
suddenly began to appreciate his poems, their airy lucidity and
lack of consequence. I think Mr Boyle thought all his efforts
were at last rewarded. He pressed books on me and wrote
fulsome comments on my work. And I longed to tell him it was
all only because of Clancy, because she was light and lucid like
the poems — because we'd lost our innocence together but kept
it, because we'd made love one wet Thursday in a secluded part
of Greenwich Park . . .

I read aloud from Mr Boyle's book, lying naked in the
sunshine on the bed. I wondered if he could have foreseen its
being read like this. Clancy wriggled at bits she liked. A lot of
the poets were obscure, little known men with names like
George Turberville and Thomas Vaux. We tried to imagine
what they had looked like and who the mistresses were they
wrote to, and where they screwed them, in four-posters or in
cornfields. Then Clancy said: 'No, they were probably not like
that at all. They were probably cold, scheming men who wanted
positions at court and wrote poems because it was the done
thing.' She would say sudden sharp, shrewd things like this as if
she couldn't help it. And I knew she was right.

'Like your Dad, you mean,' I said.

'Yes,' Clancy laughed. Then I told her how her Dad reminded
me of Henry VIII, and Clancy said there was an old hollow tree
in Greenwich Park where Henry VIII screwed Anne Boleyn.

At night, because of the heat and because we hardly moved
during the day and only tired ourselves by making love, we
would often lie awake till dawn. Clancy would tell me about her
uncle's estate in Suffolk. There was a crumbly red-brick house
with tall chimneys and a stable yard, a lawn, a walled orchard
and a decaying garden with a wood at the end. Through the
wood and across a stretch of heath was the tail of an estuary,
winding up from the sea. Marshes, river walls and oyster beds;
the smell of mud and salt. There was a tiny wooden jetty with
two rowing boats moored to it which were beached high in the
mud when the tide went out, and in hot weather, at low tide, the
sun cooked the mud so that when the water returned it was
warm and soupy for swimming. In the marshes there were

shelduck and redshanks — once she had seen an otter — and in the wood there were owls which you could hear hooting at night from the house.

When I listened to Clancy describing things in such detail I would be amazed by the fact that she'd done all these things, years ago, and I'd never even known she existed. And I'd long for the impossible — to have gone down those same paths with her, watched the same marsh birds, swum in the same muddy water when she and I were little more than infants. As she rambled on we'd hear the trains clacking to and fro along the railway. Once, just as she was talking about the owls in the wood we heard a ship hooting on the Thames. And for most of the night there'd be a strange mixture of noises from the tenement itself: radios and TVs and people arguing, an old man's cough and the sound of bottles smashing, the noise the kids made invading the stairs and the yells and threats when somebody tried to drive them out. But we hardly let this bother us, and, even in that area of London, there came a time when, while Clancy babbled, you could imagine that outside there were mud-flats and marshes and meadows with dykes and sluice-gates; just as at other times, when we'd try to remember lines from 'Romeo and Juliet' which we'd both done for 'O' level, we'd try to imagine that instead of the scrap yards and junk tips there were the piazzas and bell-towers of Verona.

'What's your uncle like?' I asked Clancy.

'He's a randy old bastard who can't do anything about it because he's stuck in a wheel-chair.' Clancy smiled. 'You'd like him, he's like you.'

I said I didn't have a wheel-chair.

'I didn't mean that.'

'How old is he?'

'Seventy-three.'

'What's he do?'

'In weather like this, he sits out in the orchard with this nurse in a bikini who brings him drinks. He used to paint a bit — watercolours — before his illness.'

I was lying on my front and Clancy was stroking the backs of my legs. I couldn't imagine myself in a wheel-chair.

'How ill is he? Seriously.'

'Pretty ill. It's the winters. It gets cold there. The house isn't in such wonderful condition, you know.' I realised that Clancy was speaking as if of some future home. 'He nearly died last winter.'

I pictured Clancy's uncle sitting out in the orchard with his voluptuous attendant, enjoying perhaps his last summer.

I said, 'Do you think he's happy?'

'I think he's happier now — since my aunt died — than he's ever been. But then he's an invalid.'

When Clancy became exhausted with talking about Suffolk she would ask me about Gauguin. I said he was a French stock-broker who gave up his job to be a painter. He left his wife and family and went to Tahiti, where he lived with a native girl, painted his greatest pictures and died, in poverty, of syphilis.

One day Clancy was gone a long while on one of her trips to the Post Office. I was worried. I thought her parents' spies had swooped at last. But then she returned, sweating, with the money, a carrier-bag of shopping and a lumpy brown paper parcel. 'Here,' she said, kissing me and taking off her blouse, 'For you.' Inside the parcel there were six assorted pots of watercolour paint and a set of three brushes.

'You ought to be a painter,' Clancy said. And after a moment's pause, '— or a poet.'

'But you shouldn't have bought this. We need the money.'

'It's my money.'

'But — I don't know how to paint. I haven't painted since I was a kid.'

'That doesn't matter. You've got the feel for it. I can see. You ought to be an artist.'

I thought of explaining to Clancy that admiring an artist or two wasn't the same as possessing their gifts.

'But what am I going to paint on? I've got nothing to paint on.'

Clancy quickly gulped down a mug of water from the sink and waved her hand. 'There's all that — and all that.' She pointed to two walls of the room from which the wallpaper had either been stripped back to the bare plaster or peeled of its own accord. 'You can use the draining board as a palette. If you like, you can paint me.' And she pulled off the rest of her clothes and bounced onto the bed, hair tossed back, one knee raised, one arm extended.

So I began to paint the walls of our room. I quickly forgot my initial doubts at Clancy's whim and made up for them with gratitude. I suppose I was really flattered and touched by the idea Clancy had of me, which only corresponded to some idea I secretly nursed of myself, as an artist, producing wonders in some garret.

My painting lacked skill, and the subjects were predictable — palm trees, paradisial fruits, lagoons, native girls in flowered sarongs, all stolen from Gauguin. But I knew what I was really painting and Clancy knew what I was really painting and what it meant. Each native girl was intended to be Clancy; and each one, it was true, was slightly less crude and ungainly than its predecessor, so that one day I really hoped to capture Clancy in paint. All through the early part of June I painted the first wall, while Clancy wrote to her uncle, describing my great talents and saying how few people truly understood life. To be happy and occupied seemed easy. You found a place of your own and made love. You rented a squalid room in Bermondsey and painted Polynesian scenes on the wall. Clancy's more extravagant fancies didn't seem to matter. Once she wrapped her arms round my neck as I cleaned my brush: 'I had a letter from Uncle today. When we go to Suffolk you'll paint there, and write poems, won't you? All the painters painted there.' I didn't answer this. As for being a poet, I didn't get beyond 'Sonnets and Lyrics of the English Renaissance'. I was content as we were.

Then things changed. Nothing fundamental altered, but a host of minor things that had never bothered us before began to affect us. The dirt of our room and the smells of the tenement which we'd been heedless of up till then because we were preoccupied with each other, began to irritate us. This was odd because it was just at the time when I was transforming out little hole into a miniature Tahiti that we began to sense the filth around us. Before, we'd tipped all our rubbish, empty tin cans, milk cartons and vegetable peelings, into old grocery boxes till they overflowed, and we'd hardly noticed the stink or the swarms of flies. Now we bickered over whose turn it was to carry the rubbish boxes down to the dustbins at street level. We felt our lack of changes of clothes, even though we seldom wore any. Before, we used to wash clothes, because it was cheaper than the launderette, in an old two-handled zinc tub we'd found propped under the sink; and we'd wash ourselves in the same way, one of us sitting in, laughing, while the other tipped water over us. Now Clancy began to hanker after showers and proper laundering. Somehow we stopped thinking the same things together and wanting to do the same things at the same time — make love, eat, sleep, talk — which had meant that in the past there was never any need for decisions or concessions. Now the slightest things became subjects for debate. We began to get insecure about being found out and dragged back to the homes we'd left, even though we'd survived for nearly three months; and at night the noises in the tenement, the scufflings and shouts on the stairs made us nervous. Clancy would start up, clutching herself — 'What's that?! What's that?!' — as if the police or some mad killer were about to burst in at the door.

Even the endless sunshine, which was such a blessing to us, began to feel stale and oppressive.

We were aware at least of one, unspoken reason for all this. Our money was dwindling. The figures in Clancy's Post Office book were getting smaller and smaller and the time was coming when we'd have to get jobs. We'd both understood that this would happen sooner or later. It wasn't so much the having to work that depressed us, but the thought that this would change us. We wanted to believe we could go out to work and still keep our desert island intact. But we knew, underneath, that work would turn us into the sort of creatures who went to work: puppets who only owned half their lives — and we'd anticipated this by stiffening already and becoming estranged from each other. Maybe this was a sort of defeatism. Clancy started looking at the job columns in newspapers. We'd existed quite happily before without newspapers. It was a sign of how different things were that I'd watch her for some time sitting with the pages spread in front of her, before asking the needless question: 'What are you doing?'

'Looking for jobs. What's it look like?'

'If anyone's going to get a job it'll be me,' I said, tapping a finger against my chest.

Clancy shook her head. 'No,' she said, licking a finger to turn over a page, 'You've got to perfect your painting. You mustn't give that up, must you?'

She really meant this.

'You're not going out to work while I piss about here,' I said, feeling I was adopting a stupid pose.

Then we had a row — Clancy accused me of betraying ideals — the upshot of which was that we both went out the next Monday looking for jobs, feeling mean and demoralised.

There was a dearth of employment, especially for school-leavers. But it was possible to find casual, menial jobs, which was all we wanted. Clancy got a job as a waitress in a pizza house near the Elephant and Castle. I went there once and bought a cup of coffee. She was dressed up in a ridiculous white outfit, with a white stiff cap with a black stripe and her hair pinned up like a nurse. On the walls of the pizza house there were murals with pseudo-Italian motifs which were worse than my pseudo-Gauguins. I looked at Clancy at the service counter and thought of her lying on the bed in the sunshine and swimming in the muddy creek in Suffolk and how she'd said: 'Paint me.' It was so depressing that when she brought me my coffee we said 'Hello' to each other as if we were slight acquaintances.

I got a job in a factory which made lawn-mowers. Bits of lawn-mower came along on moving racks and you had to tighten up the nuts with a machine like a drill on the end of a cable. This was all you did all day. It turned you into an imbecile.

Three or four weeks passed. We'd come in, tired and taciturn after work and spend the evenings getting on each other's nerves. We thought, once we left our jobs behind then we'd return to our own life. But it wasn't like that. We brought our jobs home with us as we brought home the day's sweat in our sticky clothes. Clancy was still serving frothy coffee; I was still tightening nuts. Clancy would slump on the bed and I'd stare out the window. Work seemed a process of humiliation. I looked at the scrap-heaps and demolition sites which once we'd been able to ignore, which we'd even transformed into a landscape of happiness. I thought: we'd escaped, in the midst of everything we'd escaped; but now the tower blocks and demolition sites were closing in. I made an effort to keep cheerful. I read out poems from the book and I explained to Clancy how I was going to finish my mural. But she didn't listen. She no longer seemed to care about my artistic talents. All she seemed interested in were the letters from her uncle, and when one arrived she'd read it over in a lingering, day-dreamy way and not let me look at it. It was as if she were trying to make me jealous.

Once, as I was flipping through 'Sonnets and Lyrics', I came across a poem I hadn't noticed before. 'Here,' I said, 'listen to this.' And I read aloud:

Sweet Suffolk owl, so trimly dight,
With feathers like a lady bright . . .

I thought she would like it.

She whipped the book from my hands and flung it across the room. It landed under the sink, near the zinc tub. It was a good, solid book; and it wasn't even mine. I watched the pages come away from the binding at the spine.

'It's crap! All the poems in that book are crap! Artificial, contrived crap!'

She said this with such venom that I believed her at once. A whole reservoir of delight was instantly poisoned.

'Like those paintings,' she said, getting up and gesturing. 'They're crap too! Sentimental, affected, second-hand crap! They're not even well painted!'

And at once I saw my Tahitian girls — each one a would-be Clancy — for what they really were: stumpy, stick-legged ciphers, like the drawings of a four-year-old.

'Crap, crap! All of it!'

Then she began to cry, and brushed me away when I tried to comfort her.

It was now past the middle of July. Everything was turning bad. Then, to cap matters, I had an accident with a saucepan of boiling water and scalded myself badly.

It happened needlessly and stupidly. The ledge on which our two gas rings rested was only a rickety affair, held up by wall brackets. The plaster below, into which the wall brackets were screwed, was soft and crumbly and we knew there was a danger of the ledge giving way. I kept saying to Clancy I'd fix it. One day we were making kedgeree. Clancy had put the saucepan on to boil for the rice and I was bending down to scrape something into the rubbish box which was just to the left of the gas rings. Clancy suddenly said, 'Look out!' A great chunk of plaster had fallen out of the wall and the left hand bracket was hanging on only the tips of the screws. Instead of doing the sensible thing and jumping out of the way, I reached to hold up the ledge. Just as I did so the bracket came away and most of the contents of the boiling saucepan slopped over my hands.

I did a sort of dance round the room. Clancy yelled at me to put my hands under the tap. 'Cold water! It's the best thing!' she said, trying to keep calm. But although I knew she was quite right, I didn't want to do this at first. I wanted to scream and curse and ignore Clancy and frighten her. It was a kind of revenge for her deriding my painting.

'Shit! Shit!' I said, waving my hands and hopping.

'The tap!' said Clancy.

The pain was bad at first, but it was nothing to the pain that began about an hour later and went on for hours. By this time I was sitting astride a chair by the sink, my arms plunged into cold water, my forehead pressed against the sink rim, while Clancy kept topping up the water, which would start to steam after a while, and sponged my upper arms. It wasn't pain alone, though that was bad enough. I started to feel shivery and sick — Clancy put a blanket round my shoulders. At the same time we were both silently thinking that perhaps I had a serious scald which needed proper medical treatment. This frightened and dismayed us. It wasn't just that we feared that a visit to a hospital wuld lay us open to discovery — we were already worried that our jobs might do that. It was more that going to a doctor would be a sort of admission of helplessness. Up till now everything we'd done, even getting jobs, had been done independently, of our own choosing, and hard though things had got, nothing had made us feel we couldn't survive by ourselves.

'I'm scared,' Clancy said.

'It's all right. I'll be all right,' I said, my face pressed against the wet enamel of the sink. 'I shan't go to any doctor.'

Clancy sponged my arms.

'I didn't mean it about your painting. Really. And I didn't mean to throw your book at the wall. I was just depressed.'

Most of that night we sat like that, I slumped over the sink and Clancy sponging. I was too much in pain to sleep. Whenever I took my hands from the water they felt as if they were being scalded a second time. Clancy tried to say reassuring things and now and then her hand tightened on my shoulder. We listened to the trains clacking up and down and the strange noises of the tenement. Only at about four did we attempt to go to bed, and then Clancy half filled the zinc tub with water and placed it by the bed, so that I lay on one side with my arms dangling into water — though I didn't sleep. Clancy nestled with her arm round me. I felt her doze off very quickly. I thought: in spite of the pain I'm in, in spite of our lousy jobs, in spite of everything, we are happier now, and closer than we've been for several weeks.

In the morning there were huge pearly blisters on my hands. The fingers had mostly escaped unharmed but the palms, the wrists and parts of the backs of the hands were in a hideous state. The pain had eased but the slightest touch or trying to bend my wrists brought it back instantly. Clancy got up, went out to a chemist and came back with various things in tubes and bottles including a thick, slimy cream the colour of beeswax. She made a phone call to her pizza house and gave some excuse about not coming in. The fact was that though I could waggle my fingers I could not close my blistered palms and Clancy had to spoon-feed me and literally be my hands. I knew the important thing with burns was to keep the blistered area free of infection and to let the skin repair by exposure to the air. So for two days we sat, out of the direct sunlight, my hands held out in front of us like a pair of gruesome exhibits, waiting for the blisters to go down. Things were like they were when we'd first run away and got our room.

'Will it leave a scar?' Clancy said.

'Probably,' I said.

'I won't mind.'

'Good.'

'There could be worse places for it.'

Even when, on the fourth day, Clancy went back to work (I

insisted that she did — I could just hold a spoon by this stage, and I was worried she'd lose her job if she left it any longer), the evenings were somehow special. They were not like the dull, fretful evenings we had of late. Clancy would come in, her waitress work over, and only want to know about my hands. We discussed them and fussed over them like some third thing which tied us together. It was as if we had a child. As they began to get better we started to make grim, extravagant jokes at their expense:

'The blisters'll burst and pus will go flying all round the room.'

'They'll shrivel up into nothing.'

'They'll go manky and mouldy and have to be cut off — then you'll be a cripple and I won't love you any more.'

I thought: when my hands are better, when I'm no longer an invalid — this happiness will fade.

But though, after a week, my hands were no longer very painful, it was some time — over three weeks — before the skin fully recovered and hardened. Throughout this period I sat idle in the room all day and I noticed, each evening, how Clancy's mood dulled, how she became tired again and begrudging. She saw this herself and tried to resist it. Once she came in with another brown paper parcel. It was a book — 'Love Poetry of the Seventeenth Century'. She had made a special trip in her lunch break to get it.

'It can't be much fun sitting here all by yourself all day.'

We had moved the bed permanently under the window now, and I used to sit, propped up against the metal bed-head, looking out, like some dying man on a verandah, taking his last view of the world. I thought about lots of things — in between snatches of Herrick and Crashaw — during those long, hot days. Of the lawn-mower factory — someone else would have my job by now and perhaps no one would know I'd ever been there. Of my parents and Clancy's parents; whether they really worried about us or had forgotten us. Of Gauguin dying in Tahiti. And I thought about Clancy's uncle. Clancy hadn't had a letter from him for a while (she usually had one about once a week), and this worried her. I imagined him sitting, just as I was sitting, a cripple, in his wheelchair in the sunshine. I wondered

whether he really did enthuse about Clancy and our running
away or whether it was just the foolish, romantic notion of a
tired, slightly dotty old man who couldn't move. Perhaps, in his
enthusiasm, he merely lied for Clancy's sake, because he was
really too sick and worn out to care. I thought about the money
that Clancy said he had. I didn't believe in this money. The
money of people with big houses in the country always proves
to be non-existent. Or it all gets accounted for in debts and
duties. In any case, the money made me uneasy. The more I
thought, the more suspicious and sceptical I became. I found I
couldn't imagine the orchard wall, the creek with the jetty. I
even began to believe that Clancy's uncle and his house didn't
exist; they were some fiction invented by Clancy as an incentive
— like Clancy's father imagining he was descended from the
aristocracy.

I read from the book Clancy had bought me — Lovelace,
Suckling, the Earl of Rochester — but my attention wandered. I
became irritable and sullen. I had to sit with my hands inside a
plastic carier-bag because otherwise flies would come buzzing
round settling on my cracked and blistered skin. Every time I
wanted to turn a page I had to take out my hands, wave away
the flies and use just my finger tips on the book. If I wanted to
shift my position I had to do so without using my hands. Simple
things became complicated feats. I would sit pondering the
absurdity of my position: stuck on a bed with my hands in a
polythene bag, reading Lovelace to the sound of bulldozers, half
surrounded by the painting (there was still a lot of wall to go)
which I was incapable of continuing. And from this I'd leap to
wider absurdities. What were we doing in a condemned tenement
in Bermondsey? What would become of us in the future?

'You've let the cover curl up in the sun.'

Clancy had come in. She had her tired, waitress face.

'I know,' I said. 'Sorry.'

I used to watch the school across the road; the kids coming
and going in the morning and afternoon and streaming into the
playground at breaks. It was getting near the time they broke up
for the summer; then the school would close for good and
demolition men would move in. Through one of the tall windows,
opposite but a little below our room, I could see the teacher

standing before the blackboard, but because of the level of the
window I couldn't see his seated class. It looked as if he was
speaking and gesticulating to no one. I watched him struggling
to communicate with his invisible audience, waving his arms
and raising his voice, and I felt sorry for him. He made me think
of Mr Boyle, who even now would be offering Sidney and
Spenser to the fifth year, who were more interested in Rod
Stewart and Charlton Athletic. It seemed ages since I left school,
though it was only a year. I thought of all my old school friends
and what they were doing, whether they had jobs or not. I
thought of Eddy. He'd somehow disowned me as soon as I got
interested in poetry. I wondered if there were units of the Royal
Artillery in Northern Ireland. I wondered if Eddy was sitting in
an armoured car in the Falls Road thinking of Mr Boyle.

In the third week of July the school closed and the din from
the playground ceased. Almost immediately several council
vans turned up and took away the interior furnishings. Some of
the equipment in the kitchen was dismantled and some old fold-
up desks were stacked in the playground. Then the vans drove
away, leaving the school like a forlorn fort amidst the besieging
demolition sites. I asked myself if the kids who had gone to the
school cared that it was going to be flattened. I saw some of
them sometimes, playing games over the demolition sites, rooting
about amongst the rubbish heaps, setting fire to things and
being chased off by the site workers.

Then one day, only about a fortnight after the school closed,
there were two boys in the school playground. They were
walking around, looking at the heap of desks and peering
through the wired ground-floor windows. I was puzzled as to
how they'd got there. Then I saw the head of a third boy — and
a fourth — appear over the playground wall in the far left
corner where it joined the school building. There seemed to be a
loose section of the wire netting above the wall, which could be
lifted back and squeezed under, and although the wall was a
good ten feet, the pile of desks in the corner made it possible,
even for a boy of eleven or so, to lower himself down. In a short
while there were five boys in the playground, mooching about
in grubby jeans and tee-shirts.

Their first impulse was to ransack everything. I watched them try to force their way into the school building through the big door from the playground. When this failed, they picked up some old lengths of piping left by the council workers and, poking them through the metal grilles over the windows, began smashing the panes. They used the same bits of piping to hack up lumps of asphalt from the playground, which they hurled at the upper windows. The noise they made was lost in the general noise of demolition. One of them climbed up onto the roof of one of the two small lavatory buildings abutting the school wall and, with the aid of a drain pipe, tried to reach the first floor windows — but climbed down when he realised he would be visible from street level. Then they started to dismantle the lavatories themselves — crude little temporary buildings made from flimsy prefabricated materials, with corrugated asbestos roofs.

I wondered whether these were the same kids who broke into the tenement and set fire to the litter on the stairs. They came the next day, and the day after that, and the next day again. It seemed odd that they should return at all to the school — like released prisoners going voluntarily back to prison. They stripped the lavatories bare so that the cisterns, bowls and rusty urinals were exposed, and these became the subjects of scatalogical frenzies. They started to break up some of the desks from the pile in the corner. One day I noticed them throwing about something soft and dark which they had discovered on the asphalt. They were hurling it at each other's faces and laughing. I realised it was a pigeon, a sooty-feathered London pigeon that must have fluttered very recently into the playground to die. They kept tossing it at each other; until one of them picked it up by the wing, raised it high and jerked his arm hard so that the wing came off in his hand. They all laughed. He did the same with the second wing. Then they began a mad, yelling, direction-less game of football, kicking the pigeon's body across the asphalt and against the playground walls. The grey lump of bird turned a dark, purply red. The game ended when one of the boys kicked the bird unintentionally over the playground wall. Nobody seemed interested in retrieving it.

This was on the third afternoon. After the game with the pigeon they grew listless and lethargic. They sat and sprawled about on the broken-up asphalt, now and then gouging up lumps of it and throwing them aimlessly. The sun blazed down. They looked like real prisoners now, idle and demoralised inside the high walls. I thought: they've had enough; they'll go now — their old playground holds nothing for them.

But they didn't go. They re-appeared the next morning. It was as if there had been some over-night resolution. Between them, they had a pick-axe, a shovel and a long-handled fork. Perhaps they had been stolen from one of the building sites. They began to discuss something in the near right-hand corner of the playground, looking at the ground and marking out imaginary lines with their feet. Then one of them lifted the pick-axe and, rather clumsily at first, began hacking at the asphalt. It was difficult to see all this. Even with my high vantage point, the near wall partially obscured them. But it was obvious they were digging a hole. When one had wielded the pick-axe for a few minutes another would take over, and at intervals one of them would scrape away the dislodged asphalt and earth with the shovel. The unoccupied ones sat around, looking on silently and intently.

I wondered what all this meant. By mid-day they had dug a hole deep enough to come up to their shoulders and there was a substantial heap of earth on the asphalt. Two of them went off and returned later with other tools — trowels, garden forks, a bucket. All of a sudden, I understood. They were digging a tunnel. The hole was perhaps seven or eight feet from the right hand wall. If they dug towards it and for about the same distance beyond it they would emerge in the little triangle of grass — now almost worn away or dried up by the sun — with the solitary bench on it.

I watched them work on all that afternoon and the next morning. They reached the tricky point where they had to turn the angle of the hole so that they could start to dig horizontally towards the wall. Why were they doing it? Was it a game? Had they transformed the playground, in their minds, into some prison camp, patrolled by armed guards and watch-dogs? Their task was too strenuous for a game, surely. And yet, if it wasn't a game, it was absurd: they were trying to escape from a place they had entered — and could leave — at their own free will.

Suddenly, I wanted them to succeed.

'Look Clancy —' I said. Clancy had come in from work. She had a carton of yoghurt with her. She sat down, ripped off the foil and began eating without speaking. '— a tunnel.'

Clancy looked out of the window. 'What tunnel?' All she could see was a pile of earth in the playground.

She licked at her yoghurt, bending her face over it.

'A tunnel. The kids are digging a tunnel in the playground.'

'That's a stupid thing to do.'

I didn't explain. We didn't talk much to each other in the evenings now. It seemed an effort.

For several days I watched them dig. I forgot my hands, my irritation, my uselessness. From where I sat, I could see the goal of their labours — the patch of grass to the right of the wall — whereas they could not. I surveyed their exertions like a god. But there was much that I couldn't see. I couldn't see how far the tunnel had progressed — all I could see was the expanding heaps of earth and, every few minutes, a boy emerging from the entrance hole, gasping and smeared with soil, and another taking his place. I began to have fears for them. Might the whole thing cave in? Had they dug deep enough to go beneath the foundations of the wall? How were they managing to breathe and to extract the earth as they dug? But now and then I would glimpse things that reassured me: odd bits of wood — fragments of desks and the torn-down lavatories — being used for shoring, lengths of hose-pipe, a torch, plastic bags on the ends of cords. On the asphalt over the estimated line of the tunnel they marked out a broad lane in chalk where, clearly, no one was to stand. Their ingenuity, their determination enthralled me. I remembered the pigeon they had kicked round the playground. But I worried about other things that might still thwart them. Might they run into a gas main and be forced to stop? Might they simply give up from exhaustion? And if they overcame all this, might the council men or the demolition workers arrive before they had time to finish? The more I thought of all these things, the more it seemed that their escape was real: that there was a conspiracy of forces against them and some counter-force in the boys themselves.

I did not want to imagine them failing.

I said to Clancy: 'My hands will be better soon.'

'Oh — really. That's good.'

'It could have been worse. Think of all the worse things that could have happened.'

'That's right — look on the bright side.'

We were quite apart now, wrapped in ourselves. Clancy spent all her time sweating in the pizza house or brooding over her uncle and his absent letters, and I spent all my time obsessed by the tunnel.

It was nearing the middle of August. The sun kept shining. The evening papers Clancy sometimes brought home spoke of droughts and water restrictions. People were complaining of the fine weather. They would have complained just as much if the summer had been wet. On the little triangular plot by the school the thin grass had turned a straw colour and the earth was hard and cracked. I kept watch on this patch of ground now. At any moment I expected the tunnellers to break surface. In the corner of the playground the diggers seemed to be getting excited. The nearer the moment came, the more I exaggerated the dangers of discovery and I willed the council men to delay one more day. I thought of the difficulty of digging up, entombed by earth, against the hard, baked top-soil.

And then, one afternoon, it happened. It seemed odd that it should happen, just like that, without fanfares and announcements. Suddenly, a segment of cracked soil lifted like a lid, only about five feet from the outer face of the wall. A trowel poked upwards, and a hand, and then, after a pause in which the earth lid rocked and crumbled, a head thrust into the air in a cloud of dust. It wore an expression of serene joy as if it had surfaced in a new world. It lay perched for some time on the ground, as if it had no body, panting and grinning. Then it let out a cry of triumph. I watched the head drag out shoulders and arms, and a body behind it; and then the four on the other side of the wall disappear one by one into the hole and re-appear, struggling out, on the grass triangle. No one seemed to see them — the traffic went by heedlessly, the bulldozers whined and growled. It was as if they had been transformed and were invisible. They brushed themselves down and — like climbers on a mountain peak — shook each other's hands. And then, they simply ran off — down the adjacent side street, past the boarded up shops and the empty terraces — covered in earth, clasping each other and flinging their fists ecstatically into the air.

Clancy came in about an hour later.

'Clancy,' I said, 'Clancy, I want to tell you something —' But she was waving an envelope at me, a long white envelope with black print on it. Her face was strangely agitated, as if she might be either pleased or upset.

'Look,' she said.

'Clancy, Clancy —'

'Look at this.'

She took the letter out of the envelope and placed it in front of me. It bore the heading of a firm of solicitors in Ipswich. The letter began with 'condolences' and mentioned the 'sad death' of Clancy's uncle, as if this were something that Clancy should already be aware of, and then went on to speak of 'our late client's special and confidential instructions'. The gist of it was that Clancy's uncle was dead and Clancy had been left the larger part of his money and property, subject to its being held in trust till she was twenty-one. There were vague, guarded statements about the exact scope of the legacy and a reference to 'outstanding settlements', but a meeting with Clancy was sought as soon as possible.

'Well — what do you think?'

'I'm sorry.'

'Sorry?'

'Sorry about your uncle.'

We looked at each other without speaking. I didn't know what else to say. I took Clancy's hand in my own, half-healed, scabrous hand.

I said: 'Clancy, it's your day off tomorrow. Let's go out. Let's go out and get a train to somewhere in the country, and talk.'

Personal Essay
by Graham Swift

It is hard to say — or remember! — how stories begin. Writers talk of 'ideas' for stories. In my experience it is more usual that some 'fragment' — an image, a situation, even a random sentence or phrase — enters the mind and seems to insist that it is *part* of a story. The task is then to construct or rather 'discover' that story. In 'Chemistry' the very concrete image of three figures, of different generations, beside a possibly wintry pond, with a toy boat, came long before I had any notion of the actual narrative or of how the characters related. In 'The Tunnel' the starting point was perhaps the image of a deserted, condemned school playground.

The short story, it is often said, is one of the most difficult of literary forms. Having written both novels and short stories, I know that there is at least one, fairly obvious way in which writing stories is easier. With a story your initial inspiration can carry you all the way through — you can write it all, as it were, in one breath. This is not possible with the novel. There you need staying-power and the ability to develop a long-term relationship with your material, a marriage rather than a brief affair.

A novel has the time and space to explore thoroughly a whole imagined world. A short story can only suggest a glimpse of such a world. But — and *this* is the difficulty of the short story — it must do so just as convincingly. I have noticed that a number of my stories set up for themselves 'small', enclosed, even claustrophobic worlds — they deal with houses, rooms or other locations in which a sense of confinement is strong. So too may be the desire for escape.

The effect of a short story is of course quite different from that of a novel. One of the essential processes of any novel is familiarisation. You begin with things that may initially be strange, but you learn to 'inhabit' them — one of the pleasures of novel-reading is just this feeling of entering another world and living in it as if it were your own. The short story, because it cannot offer any such gradual acclimatisation, really has an opposite function. What so many short stories have in common is that they are saying, in one form or another: 'Isn't it strange?' They are reminding us that life, even everyday life, is more peculiar, more mysterious than we often assume. They are like those actual experiences we all have — often the result of fleeting encounters — which make us feel that what we thought was familiar and straightforward is not really familiar or straightforward at all. In this respect, the written short story is not so different from the ordinary, spoken story-telling we all indulge in: 'A funny thing happened to me . . .'; 'You won't believe this, but . . .' To tell a tale is essentially to relate some strange event, and even twentieth century story-tellers should not divorce themselves from this primitive, slightly magical compulsion.

The revelation that 'things are strange' is of course exciting; it gives a drama to life that we all need. It can also be troubling and uncomfortable. The short story has great power to *disturb*. If I would not apologise for my stories often having a bizarre content, I would not apologise either for their content often being rather painful. A novel may have its shocks and crises, but these are to some extent absorbed by the novel's context and duration, the feeling of 'life going on'. In a short story, where there is not this comforting frame of reference, unsettling material may be very painful indeed. This is one reason, I think, why some readers simply find short stories 'hard to take'.

For the writer of a short story one practical but crucial difficulty is knowing how long it should be. A novel can, so to speak, be as long as it likes. It can *exhaust* its own possibilities. But because a short story *is* short its status is much less secure and everything within it is focused and conspicuous, which means that any misjudgement will declare itself at once. A story which would work superbly over five pages may be a disaster over ten, and vice versa. Knowing exactly at what point to start and end a story is a matter of some delicacy, and questions of pace, rhythm, timing and tension — the almost mathematical problem of knowing how much 'word-space' should be given to each element in the narrative — are vital.

In general, it is very hard to write a story in which there is not some sense either of 'over-spill' — the story is too long, tension and concentration are lost — or of the 'skeletal' — the narrative is so concentrated that it is abstract, it does not come to life.

I nearly always write in the first person, partly because I prefer the located, ground-level view this gives, but partly because the narrator is every bit as important to me as the narrative. I do not mean necessarily the character or personality of the narrator, because in many of my stories the narrator may actually appear as somewhat 'detached' from his experience precisely *because* he has to narrate it. It is more a case of a 'telling voice' existing in urgent relationship to what is being told.

My narrators are frequently people who have suffered some crisis, loss or revelation — life has become, for them, 'strange' and 'disturbing'. They have lost their hold on experience, and to some extent their identity. Telling the story of their crisis is their way — though it may be a fragile and illusory one, since stories, after all, are not a substitute for life — of regaining their hold on experience.

Stories exist to entertain and excite, but they are also a process of recovery, in both senses of the word — they have a therapeutic power. I believe it is important not only to tell stories but to show the *need* for their telling. In my stories, perhaps, the real 'subject' is always the story-teller.

ROGER MAIS

Lunch Hour Rush

The vacant tables were filling up rapidly. The hum of conversation grew steadily in volume. A Ham-and-Eggs over by the window camouflaged himself behind a newspaper and watched the pageant of feminine legs crossing and recrossing the busy street below. He was a connoisseur of feminine pulchritude from the waist down. He was past middle age, bald on top, and a bachelor.

'Coffee or dessert?'

He raised his eyes to those of the little waitress who effervesced with latent energy.

'Coffee. Black.'

As Milly turned briskly to another table, his eyes raked her fore and aft. This girl was a knowing one. She never came near enough to enable him to pinch her under cover of the tablecloth. On one occasion he had asked her to turn the window so as to manoeuvre her between the table and the wall. She would have to come close then, because she was not tall enough to reach the window otherwise. He could place the newspaper carelessly in such a position as to cover the stealthy approach of his hand . . . but Milly had unexpectedly come all the way round the table, approaching the window from the other side. This little manoeuvre on her part had entirely upset all his carefully arranged plans. He had been outflanked, defeated. A smart little girl was Milly. He had tried to cover up his chagrin with a short laugh.

Milly was on her toes now. She was the smartest, most popular waitress in the place. She got the most tips, the biggest ones. But if she kept on like this she would have a nervous breakdown. In spite of her occasional dizzy-spells she had to keep on being as bright as a new sixpence, courteous, quick. She had always to keep her wits about her too.

She had her regular customers who waited for her to come and get their orders, and there were new customers dropping in all the while who kept crooking their fingers at her and trying to catch her eye.

The Usual, over by the left wing, was sometimes very trying. He was a vegetarian with a sour face and disposition, as though life disagreed with him. He complained about something or the other two out of three times. His tips, when they did come, were a couple of coppers at the most.

Then there were the two typists who although they worked in different buildings, always met at lunch time, generally at their own special table. One would not order until the other arrived. The moment they got together they acted as though they were old school friends who had not met in years and were overwhelmed with joy at this chance encounter, they had so much to tell each other, they talked so excitedly with so many 'my dear's' and giggles. One could hardly wait for the other to finish a sentence. It seemed too they did not care who overheard what they said, so that by the odd bits of sentences let fall in her presence, Milly, if she had had the desire, could have reconstructed the biographies of those two city typists with scarcely an effort.

'. . . my dear, I am certain he said Colon — not Columbia. He'll be taking the plane, of course, and he has promised to write me everyday by air-mail. Do you think my organdie would look well trimmed with green?'

'How are you making it? I saw Elsie with something terrific with green taffeta trimmings. And that reminds me about "Bold Aventure" . . . I don't mean the racehorse . . .'

A transient Hamburger Steak caught Milly's eye and crooked a beckoning finger in her direction. Milly answered his flattering eyes with a non-committal smile. Milly thought: 'I am going to ask him for the last time this evening, just as he is through checking the cash. I'm going to put it squarely to him — no nonsense . . . and if he tries to get fresh with me again I'll slap his face this time, job or no job. And if he says "No," I'm going to ask for two weeks leave to go the country. If I get it, it will be without pay, but I need the rest, and Phil and I can do some close figuring in those two weeks . . .'

The Hamburger Steak gave her a shilling extra.

'For yourself,' he said, and held her hand for an instant as she took the money from him.

Milly smiled her most non-committal smile. 'Thank you.'

'Doing anything tonight?'

'Nothing special. But I expect the boyfriend will be around as usual. We may go to a show, or just sit on our own bit of porch and hold hands.'

She paused for an instant at the table of the Usual, and noted the mess of herbs seemed to please him for once. He even spared her a sort of smile, embellished with a quivering lettuce leaf.

One of her late customers was coming in. He was early today. He wore his usual absent-minded air, but Milly could tell that something unusual had happened. Something exciting. His smile was a little less impersonal, his eyes didn't look quite so tired . . .

'Congratulations,' said Milly.

He warmed to her immediately. His smile was really attractive now. It subtly deprived his face of years of accumulated lines, making him seem younger, more full of beans.

'Thank you, Milly. It took a long time coming, but you know, now that it has happened it makes one feel it was well worth waiting for.'

She didn't know what in the world he was talking about, of course, what it was that had happened, but what difference did it make!

It was not until she returned with the soup that he realised this girl couldn't possibly know the nature of his good-fortune. He asked her point-blank: 'Why did you congratulate me just now?'

She answered him with a smile — the one she reserved for her friends.

'Oh I don't know. I just saw you looking happy, that's all. Does it matter?'

He laughed outright, taking a small memo-book from his pocket.

'Do you mind if I make a note of this? You see, I'm a writer. I have just have my first book accepted.'

She said: 'How splendid!' Then after a pause: 'Here's something else you might put in your book. I once said the same thing to a man simply because he was wearing a new suit of clothes — you know, cut differently, and all that. It gave him a new personality. He positively blushed, and looked self-conscious when he tried to smile. I learnt after that he had just lost his wife!'

She went away before he had time to fully digest the point of her little story.

'…my dear, he said the most delicious thing to me, and would you believe it, he danced the next *three* numbers in succession with her! I made Jerry take me to the bar just to see what was going on between them, and there they were together as thick as thieves. She's a brassy little bitch, that's what!' To Milly: 'Have you got Cherry Sundae on the menu today? Or shall we share a Banana Split? I couldn't go a whole one of those things myself. You know, I weighed last Tuesday, and was positively horrified to find I had put on three pounds, and it's all around the waistline. Very well then, make it two small Cherry Sundaes. Everytime I think of a Cherry Sundae I remember Dickie.. Don't you remember Dickie…the time with Gerald, out at Palm Beach? The same time when Muriel filled her shoe with sand and poured it down his back. Did I ever tell you what happened afterwards between Muriel and the Dennis boy? I got it from Gladys — no, not Boysie's Gladys — who use to be friendly with Bertie Simmonds while his wife was away in the country…'

Ham-and-Eggs was dawdling over his black coffee. He crooked a finger in Milly's direction, but she feigned not to see him. She was hurrying to take the orders of five young lawyers who always occupied a large table in the centre. If their table was taken before they arrived, they would push two smaller ones together. They talked and laughed loud enough to be heard by the lunchers around them. Their jokes were not exactly 'drawing-room', and their subtlest wit usually had to do with sexy matters — but they didn't try to date her or pinch her. They didn't address their remarks to her directly, though they were not above speaking *at* her, obliquely, their real meaning thinly veiled beneath a veneer of what passed in their particular circle for wit. They were not really altogether vicious — most of them.

It hurt, rather than annoyed her. Somehow she felt sorry for these jaded, unhappy young men. She smiled mechanically in response to their indirect sallies, took their orders mechanically too, as though she were thinking about something else.

She was too, she was thinking about Phil, and what she was going to say to the boss that very evening. Either he would give her that raise of pay, or she would try to find another job. She wasn't going to stand any nonsense from him, either. Phil was becoming impatient. His manner of late was irritable and his moods unpredictable. He wanted to get married. On his salary alone they could not afford it. But he was all for her leaving the restaurant and taking a shot at it. She was businesslike, though, and careful. They must save a substantial nest-egg first. She could save next to nothing on her present pay.

Either he would give her that long promised raise, or she would ask for two weeks leave. She could get a doctor's certificate to show that she needed the rest . . . those dizzy-spells . . . she was tired, she needed those two weeks anyway.

A friend of hers had found lucrative work in a beauty parlour. There were other things a girl with her looks and abilities could do, other jobs she could get. Although she had never done any other job or work than waiting in a restaurant, she had a high school education and had been training for teaching. She had taken this job because, staying in the city with relatives none too well off, just after leaving college, the necessity of securing employment had become increasingly imperative. She had had to forgo her ambitions, for the time being, she told herself, and take the first job that presented itself. Ever after that she had been too busy, or too tired to think about anything else.

And then she met Phil. Phil was a mechanic. He worked at a garage where the hours were long and the pay small, quite insufficient to keep them both. When he asked for a raise of pay the management spoke darkly of certain impending reductions to the staff on the grounds of retrenchment, which never materialised. If they could save enough money for Phil to open a shop, now, things would be different. It was their only hope as far as she could see . . . unless they could find somebody willing to put up the capital . . .

'. . . I just had to put him in his place, my dear. I told him off properly. Made him understand that he was not my boss. I have had occasion to report him to the boss twice before. He'd better watch his step, he's got a wife and two children, and I reminded him. That's three good reasons why he should want to hang on to his job with his teeth, instead of trying to order me about and tell me what I ought to do. "Miss Ainsworth," he says through his false teeth, which never seem to be quite secure in his mouth, "these returns will have to be typed over." "Typed over by who?" I asked him, just like that. He gets very red in the face like a turkey-cock. "I couldn't think of sending them to Head Office like that," he says, throwing them at me. "Don't know what New York would think we were paying typists' salaries for," he says, while I just went on powdering my nose, ignoring him. "If I pass returns like that," he says, getting redder and redder, "I'll soon be out of a job." I started laughing then and that made him all the madder. "You'll be out of a job quicker if you don't learn to behave like a gentleman." I said, and he gave *such* a look; I nearly *died* laughing.'

Milly turned away from the table and started down the passage with a tray of empties. Suddenly, unaccountably she felt light-headed, as though she would like to giggle, for no particular reason. And again that spasm of dizziness . . . She thought: Supposing everything should start going round and round the way it sometimes did when she had these spells badly — and she should fall with that tray of plates and dishes right in the middle of this place full of people! Wouldn't that be funny? She leaned against a concrete column for a moment; not so much because of the giddiness, as in order to enable her to get control over that terrible desire to laugh outright and to send the tray spinning away from her with a clatter to the tiled floor . . . or right in the lap of Ham-and-Eggs over yonder. With a well directed putt she could manage it . . . her arm gave a little involuntary twitch at the shoulder . . . and then through the corner of her eye she saw Phil come in. She held her breath slowly, and took her lower lip between her teeth.

Phil's face looked odd. Something had happened to him. She had never seen him look like this before. She swallowed hard . . . Phil needed someone to take care of him. He wasn't even eating properly these days, not enough to keep an infant going . . . She would put it to him squarely this very evening. It didn't matter now if he should fire her then and there. Phil came first — he needed her. She would say 'yes' and they could get married at the Registry as soon as he wanted. She would get another job — a better one she was sure. Either he raised her pay, or . . .

Walking firmly now, brave in the strength of her new resolve, she went across to Phil to take his order. He didn't look up. It was as though he was afraid to meet her eyes.

'Order, sir?' she said, playfully.

'Hell, Milly . . . !' He turned a haggard face to her, and looked away again.

Her own face suddenly blanched. Before he said it she had guessed.

'What is it, Phil? You can tell me the worst,' she said, calmly. 'Together we can take it, no matter how bad . . .'

Her hand trembled with the desire to touch his unruly hair, there was a physical tightening of her breasts to have his face crushed against them.

'Well, it's just as bad as you think.'

'You mean . . . ?'

'Yes, they gave me the boot. Same old story — retrenching!'

She passed a weary hand across her forehead, pushing back a stray strand of hair that flirted about her cheek.

Two tables away the Usual was cocking an imperative finger at her. He wanted his bill.

'Be back in a minute,' she said, laying a hand on his arm.

'That spinach was damn rotten,' said the Usual, grimly.

'Did you enjoy the vegetable salad, sir?' mechanically.

'Br-r-r-rh!'

She was glad to get away to the next customer who awaited her. So Phil had lost his job. Funny that she had never considered that possibility, had not therefore been able to shape her plans against such a contingency. She'd have to revise all her ideas now, of course. She couldn't go to the boss with her ultimatum as she had planned. That was out. She'd have to hang on to this job with her teeth now. Till something turned up . . .

Ham-and-Egg's leering face just didn't register on her consciousness now. She went up to the table like one who moved in a trance, and started loading her tray with empty plates, dishes. He took a generous portion of her flesh between his finger and thumb under cover of the newspaper . . .

'Don't do that!' she said, sharply. She looked at him as though she would like to dump the tray with its load of dishes right on top of his bald head. For a moment only, the look she gave him was frightening in its ferocity. The next moment she had recovered control of herself. She was smiling at him, even. The first and last rule of the restaurant was that you must be civil to the customers.

She said, coyly: 'You shouldn't do that, sir. It makes me black-and-blue there. Then I won't be able to wear my new bathing suit to the beach Sunday morning, the boyfriend isn't colour-blind, you know . . .'

Had to be civil to the customers. What did it matter to the management if a girl's bottom was pinched once in a while?

He laughed and tipped her generously. She looked at him coquettishly . . . made round-eyes at him . . .

'H-m-m-m! If that's what a gal gets for being pinched . . .!'

Yes, she had a way with men. Of course, that was what made her of value to the boss. She was the best waitress in the place. Pretty, capable, quick, uncomplaining . . . and she'd got a way with the male customers.

Again that horrible dizziness . . . She really needed the vacation badly, but she would not dare to ask for it now. Too risky.

Balancing the tray she walked easily, gracefully between the tables . . . she lurched against one of them, the one where five young men sat. Somebody laughed. She tried to steady herself with a hand on the back of a chair. Everybody seemed to be staring at her, wondering if she were drunk. Somebody said: 'Hi, Milly . . .!' and something else — she didn't hear the last part of the sentence. The chairs and tables were going round and round in a whirl. This would not do, she must get a grip of

herself . . . Somebody laughed . . . The chairs and tables did a
wild dance before her eyes . . . she was falling, falling . . .

The crash of the plates and dishes clattering against the tiled
floor created quite a stir among the lunchers. It brought the boss
himself from his office.

'Take her in my room,' he said generously, to Phil and the
man who called himself a writer, as they lifted her up from the
floor. He held the swing-door of his private office open for them
himself. There was a couch inside. They laid her upon the
couch, and somebody telephoned for a doctor.

'What she needs is rest,' the boss confided to Phil, in the tone
of one who knows about these things, 'a good long rest. Luckily
I had a likely looking girl from the country in here this very
morning looking for a job — pretty too. I have her name and
address down on my memo-pad somewhere. I must get in touch
with her right away . . . When she gets well again, maybe . . .
we'll see what we can do for her anyway . . .

'Now where the hell did I put that memo-pad?'

FRANK SARGESON

An Affair of the Heart

At Christmastime our family always went to the beach. In those days there weren't the roads along the Gulf that there are now, so father would get a carrier to take our luggage down to the launch steps. And as my brother and I would always ride on the cart, that was the real beginning of our holidays.

It was a little bay a good distance out of the harbour that we'd go to, and of course the launch trip would be even more exciting than the ride on the carrier's cart. We'd always scare mother beforehand by telling her it was sure to be rough. Each year we rented the same bach and we'd stay right until our school holidays were up. All except father who used to have only a few days' holiday at Christmas. He'd give my brother and me a lecture about behaving ourselves and not giving mother any trouble, then he'd go back home. Of course we'd spend nearly all our time on the beach, and mother'd have no more trouble with us than most mothers are quite used to having.

Well, it's all a long time ago. It's hard now to understand why the things that we occupied our time over should have given us so much happiness. But they did. As I'll tell you, I was back in that bay not long ago, and for all that I'm well on in years I was innocent enough to think that to be there again would be to experience something of that same happiness. Of course I didn't experience anything of the kind. And because I didn't I had some reflections instead that gave me the very reverse of happiness. But this is by the way. I haven't set out to philosophise. I've set out to tell you about a woman who lived in a bach not far beyond that bay of ours, and who, an old woman now, lives there to this day.

As you can understand, we children didn't spend all our time on our own little beach. When the tide was out we'd go for walks round the rocks, and sometimes we'd get mother to go with us. My brother and I would be one on each side of her, holding her hands, dragging her this way and that. We'd show her the wonders we'd found, some place where there were sea-eggs underneath a ledge, or a pool where the sea-anemones grew thick.

It was one of these times when we had mother with us that we walked further round the rocks than we had ever been before. We came to a place where there was a fair-sized beach, and there, down near low-water mark, was the woman I've spoken about. She was digging for pipis, and her children were all round her scratching the sand up too. Every now and then they'd pick up handfuls of pipis and run over near their mother, and drop the pipis into a flax kit.

Well, we went over to look. We liked pipis ourselves, but there weren't many on our own beach. The woman hardly took any notice of us, and we could have laughed at the way she was drssed. She had on a man's old hat and coat, and the children were sketches too. There were four of them, three girls and a boy; and the boy, besides being the smallest and skinniest, looked the worst of all because he was so badly in need of a hair-cut.

The woman asked mother if she'd like some pipis to take home. She said she sold pipis and mussels. They made good soup, she said. Mother didn't buy any but she said she would some other day, so the woman slung the kit on her shoulder, and off she went towards a tumble-down bach that stood a little way back from the beach. The children ran about all round her, and the sight made you think of a hen that was out with her chicks.

Of course going back round the rocks we talked about the woman and her children. I remember we poked a bit of fun at the way they were dressed, and we wondered why the woman wanted to sell us pipis and mussels when we could have easily got some for ourselves.

Perhaps they're poor, mother said.

That made us leave off poking fun. We didn't know what it was to be poor. Father had only his wages, and sometimes when we complained about not getting enough money to spend, he asked what we thought would happen to us if he got the sack. We took it as a joke. But this time there was something in what mother said that made us feel a little frightened.

Well, later on my brother and I made lots of excursions as far as that beach, and gradually we got to know the woman and her children, and saw inside their bach. We'd go home in great excitement to tell mother the things we'd found out. The woman was Mrs Crawley. She lived there all the year round, and the children had miles to walk to school. They didn't have any father, and Mrs Crawley collected pipis and mussels and sold them, and as there were lots of pine trees along the cliffs she gathered pine cones into sugar bags and sold them too. Another way she had of getting money was to pick up the kauri gum that you found among the sea-weed at high-tide mark, and sell that. But it was little enough she got all told. There was a road not very far back from the beach, and about once a week she'd collect there the things she had to sell, and a man who ran a cream lorry would give her a lift into town. And the money she got she'd spend on things like flour and sugar, and clothes that she bought in second-hand shops. Mostly, though, all there was to eat was the soup from the pipis and mussels, and vegetables out of the garden. There was a sandy bit of garden close by the bach. It was ringed round with tea-tree brush to keep out the wind, and Mrs Crawley grew kumaras and tomatoes, drum-head cabbages and runner beans. But most of the runner beans she'd let go to seed, and shell for the winter.

It was all very interesting and romantic to me and my brother. We were always down in the dumps when our holidays were over. We'd have liked to camp at our bach all the year round, so we thought the young Crawleys were luckier than we were. Certainly they were poor, and lived in a tumble-down bach with sacking nailed on the walls to keep the wind out, and slept on heaps of fern sewn into sacking. But we couldn't see anything wrong with that. We'd have done it ourselves any day. But we could see that mother was upset over the things we used to tell her.

Such things shouldn't be, she'd say. She'd never come to visit the Crawleys, but she was always giving us something or other that we didn't need in our bach to take round to them. But Mrs Crawley never liked taking the things that mother sent. She'd rather be independent, she said. And she told us there were busybodies in the world who'd do people harm if they could.

One thing we noticed right from the start. It was that Mrs Crawley's boy Joe was her favourite. One time mother gave us a big piece of Christmas cake to take round, and the children didn't happen to be about when we got there, so Mrs Crawley put the cake away in a tin. Later on my brother let the cat out of the bag. He asked one of the girls how she liked the cake. Well, she didn't know anything about it, but you could tell by the way Joe looked that he did. Mrs Crawley spoilt him, sure enough. She'd bring him back little things from town when she never brought anything back for the girls. He didn't have to do as much work as any of the girls either, and his mother was always saying, Come here Joe, and let me nurse you. It made us feel a bit uncomfortable. In our family we never showed our feelings much.

Well, year after year we took the launch to our bay, and we always looked forward to seeing the Crawleys. The children shot up the same as we did. The food they had kept them growing at any rate. And when Joe was a lanky boy of fifteen his mother was spoiling him worse than ever. She'd let him off work more and more, even though she never left off working herself for a second. And she was looking old and worn out by that time. Her back was getting bent with so much digging and picking up pine cones, and her face looked old and tired too. Her teeth were gone and her mouth was sucked in. It made her chin stick out until you thought of the toe of a boot. But it was queer the way she never looked old when Joe was there. Her face seemed to go young again, and she never took her eyes off him. He was nothing much to look at we thought, but although my brother and I never spoke about it we both somehow understood how she felt about him. Every day she spent digging in her garden or digging up pipis, pulling up mussels from the reefs or picking up pine cones; and compared to our mother she didn't seem to have much of a life. But it was all for Joe, and so long as she had Joe what did it matter? She never told us that, but we knew all the same. I don't know how much my brother understood about it, because as I've said we never said anything to each other. But I felt a little bit frightened. It was perhaps the first time I understood what deep things there could be in life. It was easy to see how mad over Joe Mrs Crawley was, and evidently when you went mad over a person like that you didn't take much account of their being nothing to look at. And perhaps I felt frightened because there was a feeling in me that going mad over a person in that way could turn out to be quite a terrible thing.

Anyhow, the next thing was our family left off going to the bay. My brother and I were old enough to go away camping somewhere with our cobbers, and father and mother were sick of the bother of going down to the bay. It certainly made us a bit sorry to think that we wouldn't be seeing the Crawleys that summer, but I don't think we lost much sleep over it. I remember that we talked about sending them a letter. But it never got beyond talk.

What I'm going to tell you about happened last Christmas. It was twenty odd years since I'd been in the bay and I happened to be passing near.

I may as well tell you that I've not been what people call a success in life. Unlike my brother who's a successful business man, with a wife and a car and a few other ties that successful men have, I've never been able to settle down. Perhaps the way I'd seen the Crawleys live had an upsetting influence on me. It's always seemed a bit comic to me to see people stay in one place all their lives and work at one job. I like meeting different people and tackling all sorts of jobs, and if I've saved up a few pounds it's always come natural to me to throw up my job and travel about a bit. It gets you nowhere, as people say, and it's a sore point with my mother and father who've just about ceased to own me. But there are lots of compensations.

Well, last Christmas Day I was heading up North after a job

I'd heard was going on a fruit-farm, and as I was short of money at the time I was hoofing it. I got the idea that I'd turn off the road and have a look at the bay. I did, and had a good look. But it was a mistake. As I've said the kick that I got was the opposite to what I was expecting, and I came away in a hurry. It's my belief that only the very toughest sort of people should ever go back to places where they've been happy.

Then I thought of the Crawleys. I couldn't believe it possible they'd be living on their beach still, but I felt like having a look. (You can see why I've never been a success in life. I never learn from my mistakes, even when I've just made them.)

I found that the place on the road where Mrs Crawley used to wait for a lift into town had been made into a bus terminus, and there was a little shelter shed and a store. All the way down to the beach baches had been built, and lots of young people were about in shorts. And I really got the shock of my life when I saw the Crawleys' bach still standing there; but there it was, and except for a fresh coat of Stockholm tar it didn't look any different.

Mrs Crawley was in the garden. I hardly recognised her. She'd shrivelled up to nothing, and she was fixed in such a bend that above the waist she walked parallel to the ground. Her mouth had been sucked right inside her head, so her chin stuck out like the toe of a boot more than ever. Naturally she didn't know me, I had to shout to make her hear, and her eyes were bad too. When I'd told her I was Freddy Coleman, and she'd remembered who Freddy Coleman was, she ran her hands over my face as though to help her know whether or not I was telling the truth.

Fancy you coming, she said, and after I'd admired the garden and asked her how many times she'd put up a fresh ring of tea-tree brush, she asked me inside.

The bach was much the same. The sacking was still nailed up over the places where the wind came in, but only two of the fern beds were left. One was Mrs Crawley's and the other was Joe's, and both were made up. The table was set too, but covered over with tea-towels. I didn't know what to say. It was all too much for me. Mrs Crawley sat and watched me, her head stuck forward, and I didn't know where to look.

It's a good job you came early, she said. If you'd come late you'd have given me a turn.

Oh, I said.

Yes, she said. He always comes late. Not till the last bus.

Oh, I said, I suppose you mean Joe.

Yes, Joe, she said. He never comes until the last bus.

I asked her what had become of the girls, but she took no notice. She went on talking about Joe and I couldn't follow her, so I got up to leave. She offered me a cup of tea, but I said no thank you. I wanted to get away.

You've got Joe's Christmas dinner ready for him, I said, and I touched the table.

Yes, she said, I've got him everything that he likes. And she took away the tea-towels. It was some spread. Ham, fruit, cake, nuts, everything that you can think of for Christmas. It was a shock after the old days. Joe was evidently making good money, and I felt a bit envious of him.

He'll enjoy that, I said. What line's he in, by the way?

He'll come, she said. I've got him everything that he likes. He'll come.

It was hopeless, so I went.

Then, walking back to the road I didn't feel quite so bad. It all came back to me about how fond of Joe Mrs Crawley had been. She hadn't lost him at anyrate. I thought of the bach all tidied up, and the Christmas spread, and it put me in quite a glow. I hadn't made a success of my life, and the world was in a mess, but here was something you could admire and feel thankful for. Mrs Crawley still had her Joe. And I couldn't help wondering what sort of a fellow Joe Crawley had turned out.

Well, when I was back on the road again a bus hadn't long come in, and the driver was eating a sandwich. So I went up to him.

Good-day, I said. Can you tell me what sort of a fellow Joe Crawley is?

Joe Crawley, he said, I've never seen him.

Oh, I said. Been driving out here long?

He told me about five years, so I jerked my thumb over towards the beach.

Do you know Mrs Crawley? I asked him.

Do I what! he said. She's sat in that shed waiting for the last bus every night that I can remember.

He told me all he knew. Long ago, people said, Joe would come several times a year, then he'd come just at Christmas. When he did come it would be always on the last bus, and he'd be off again first thing in the morning. But for years now he hadn't come at all. No one knew for sure what he used to do. There were yarns about him being a bookmaker, some said he'd gone to gaol, others that he'd cleared off to America. As for the girls they'd married and got scattered, though one was supposed to write now and then. Anyhow, wet or fine, summer or winter, Mrs Crawley never missed a night sitting in that shelter shed waiting to see if Joe'd turn up on the last bus. She still collected pine cones to sell, and would drag the bags for miles; and several times, pulling up mussels out on the reefs she'd been knocked over by the sea, and nearly drowned. Of course she got the pension, but people said she saved every penny of it and lived on the smell of an oil-rag. And whenever she did buy anything she always explained that she was buying it for Joe.

Well, I heard him out. Then I took to the road. I felt small. All the affairs of the heart that I had had in my life, and all that I had seen in other people, seemed petty and mean compared to this one of Mrs Crawley's. I looked at the smart young people about in their shorts with a sort of contempt. I thought of Mrs Crawley waiting down there in the bach with her wonderful Christmas spread, the bach swept out and tidied, and Joe's bed with clean sheets on all made up ready and waiting. And I thought of her all those years digging in the garden, digging for pipis, pulling up mussels and picking up cones, bending her body until it couldn't be straightened out again, until she looked like a new sort of human being. All for Joe. For Joe who'd never been anything much to look at, and who, if he was alive now, stayed away while his mother sat night after night waiting for him in a bus shelter shed. Though, mind you, I didn't feel like blaming Joe. I knew how he'd been spoilt, and I remembered how as a boy I'd sort of understood the way Mrs Crawley felt towards him might turn out to be quite a terrible thing. And sure enough, it had. But I never understood until last Christmas Day, when I was walking northwards to a job on a fruit-farm, how anything in the world that was such a terrible thing, could at the same time be so beautiful.

MOY McCRORY

Memento Mori

Rose used to have a boxer dog. A large brown creature with a square head, bow legs and a pigeon chest. It had been the runt of its litter which is why Rose ended up with it. She was always a soft touch where animals were concerned.

'I can't bear to see anything suffer,' she told her husband whenever she carried in another stray cat, preferably when it had been run down by a bus or was similarly afflicted.

'I only wish you'd show the same concern for me,' he said with regularity.

'You're not in dire straits like these are,' came the timed response and Eric, always on cue, said that he would have to die first before he got any sympathy.

'If I took ill you wouldn't have time to notice with all the strays you keep bringing back with you. One more and it will be me that leaves home!'

But Rose kept bringing dogs, cats, tortoises, in fact, anything the neighbours wanted rid of, Rose always obliged and he continued to say 'one more, and it will be me that leaves.'

When Rex was about twelve he died. Rose came down in the morning to find him stretched out on the sofa.

'Come on boy!' she called, patting her thigh. Getting no response, she took his lead from the hall stand. He really was sleeping heavily she thought. It must be because he was getting so old. She slipped her hand under his collar to attach the chain and as her fingers touched cold inert hide, her eyes widened. There was no other movement. With a sickening realisation Rose ran upstairs to wake her husband.

'Eric!' she called as she reached the top. 'Eric!'

She flung the door open but there was no reply. He was sleeping heavily, grey hairs beginning to crowd out the dark falling against the stark white of the pillow where his head lay. His mouth hung loosely open in an attitude of disrespect. She went to shake him but stopped midway. Her hand drew back without touching him in a horrid flash of *déjà vu*.

Later that day Eric transferred the dog into the parlour, carrying the animal across his arms and shutting the door on it. Back in the kitchen he wiped his forehead and ran hot water over his hands.

'Trust him to die when the bloody binmen are on strike,' he said, vigorously soaping himself. The entire cleansing department were on a stoppage following an overtime dispute. 'Unsociable hours, unsociable labour and an unsociable workforce' ran the waggish headlines in the local paper and although the strike was in its early stage, no one had any great confidence that it would be resolved quickly, at least not before the rubbish was piling up in the streets.

'Wait until next weekend with the sodding flies round here and that thing in the parlour.'

'You've no respect,' Rose sobbed.

'Respect!' he shouted snatching at the roller towel. 'Good God! I'd have had to slip the binmen a fiver at least to take it away, but God knows what we're going to do now! We can't dig a hole in the park for him you know, it's a health hazard,' he added sardonically. 'I'll have to take him down to the knackers yard.'

In the gloomy kitchen Rose's face alone stood out, for it had turned ashen. Across her mind the awful vision of her husband had passed, gleefully rubbing his hands as Rex was ground into bone meal. Dancing a strange festive rite in a circle around the public incinerator, cackling like one of the Macbeth witches.

'He was such a noble dog,' she sniffed, beginning to cry into her handkerchief.

'Oh bloody hell! I can see us ending up with a funeral cortege and wreaths. Well don't expect the neighbours to draw their curtains. If you ask me, there will be a lot happier faces round here once they know that that thing is dead. I honestly don't know why we didn't get more complaints than we did, the way it used to bark and howl. It must have kept people awake at night.'

'You never liked him! You never did! You were mean to him . . .' she clasped the handkerchief tightly to her mouth.

'Look Rose, I don't care how he goes. If you want to hire the Scotch Guard to beat time as he's carried out, that's up to you. But we have got to get shot of it. I'll take him tomorrow.'

Rose lifted her face and fixed him with a watery stare.

'Over my dead body!' she said.

For two days Rex leant against the piano.

'Don't you touch him!' Rose said whenever Eric went towards the parlour door. 'I'll do it.'

And each evening when he came home from work Eric asked 'Well? Has it gone yet?' Seeing Rose shake her head he would repeat his warning. 'If it hasn't gone by Thursday, so help me I'll lift it out myself and set fire to it.'

Rose did not know what to do.

After five days she phoned the police.

In Granby Street police station the desk officer picked up the telephone wearily. It was nearly the end of his shift, he had been on duty since nine the previous evening.

'You want to report a dead dog?' he repeated slowly chewing on his pencil. When did you see it and which street was it on?'

There was a pause while he tapped the pencil's end rhythmically on the note pad in front of him . . . 'O CAN YOU WASH YOUR FATHER'S SHIRT O CAN YOU WASH IT CLEAN . . .'

'I'm not sure that I understand . . . you found a dead dog on your sofa when you came down for breakfast. Did you notice anything else unusual?'

With his right hand he drew out a grid and began to fill it in with noughts and then crosses. He only had three quarters of an hour left to do before going home. Bacon and eggs, he thought, being a man of direct if rather basic thought. Maybe a sausage?

Yes, why not. He wondered if there were any beans. Just a small tin from the pantry. He wouldn't open a large one just for himself. And a bit of fried bread with some black pudding. If there was any left that was. He could pick up some from the butchers on his way home. MacCawley's made their own on the premises. He began to salivate imagining it hanging up in loops in the window.

'Pardon? Yes I do know that the binmen are on strike but it's good of you to remind me.' He realised with a jolt the matter he was attending to. 'You don't think they had anything to do with it do you?' he asked. 'Ah, yes, I think I see. It's leaning against the piano. What do you mean your husband carried it? But you should never disturb evidence.'

He began to write laboriously: 'Dog found leaning on piano.'

He went back and altered it so it read 'Dog found dead, leaning on piano.' Then he drew a line through 'dead' and moved it to the start of the sentence. There was something decidedly funny going on.

'Are you sure you're telling me everything?' he asked, wanting to follow the correct procedure for gleaning information. He tried to recall the policy. 'Normally we don't deal with dead dogs,' he said in his official voice, 'not unless they're causing an obstruction. Say you found one blocking the road, then we'd remove it or . . .' he tried to remember the other cause, 'or if they are a risk to public health. Now, would you consider this dog to be a risk — threatening, or otherwise, to the environment?'

Rose thought for a second. Mrs Furlong's dog had been a risk, they had had to have it muzzled and she had to pay thirty shillings to the police station as a fine. What on earth would they charge her for Rex? She had an irrational fear of the police force. Anyone in a uniform symbolised authority to Rose, even the usherettes in the Rialto creeping up with their red torches made Rose feel guilty. She broke out in a sweat. She didn't want them coming round for the dog and her being dragged out into the street as the owner of something that threatened the community, upbraided for being irresponsible.

'It's all right officer,' she heard herself saying. 'It's gone,' and she slammed the phone down.

Rose was overfond of animals she knew. They were her weakness. Animals and babies. And now that their only daughter had left she felt all the more need to fill their home with young living things, even if it did mean that eventually they grew old and died on her. She wished she had had more than one child, it was her deepest regret. If she could go back . . . but then, that was impossible and what was the point of thinking about it?

Eric was seventeen years older than her. He had been a widower when she had first met him. Everyone had frowned upon them then, but she didn't care. He had been good to her and if their union had not been so fruitful as they both might have wished, it was her only regret and she considered herself lucky. Eric had always been fearfully proud of Rose and he delighted in the way she was always well turned out.

'I don't know,' he always said, 'you see some women walking around with curlers in and carpet slippers as if they can't be bothered with themselves. It's a shame that they should feel so insignificant.'

Rose had always been flattered by his obvious pride in her and she did care for his opinion, so that morning, dressed in her neatly pressed black suit for the occasion, she unlocked the parlour door.

There was a slight smell but then the room was musty anyway because it was so seldom used and never heated. In the fireplace stood a bowl of greying plastic tulips with a fan of pleated paper in front of it. The room had the cold disused look of rooms that were only ever used for laying out the dead, or storing unwanted furniture. Her sewing machine was packed to one side, a sturdy black treadle from the secondhand shop that she had given fifteen shillings for. Although still in working order it was impossible to get at. The cast iron base had tins of paint and boxes of tools piled up on it. Even the piano was loaded up with debris: coffee jars full of nails, buttons, and old bits of rusted metal implements gave it the appearance of a counter in a do-it-yourself shop. It was not a room to sit in, or stand in too long for that matter. Rose hated it.

She lifted the stiffening Rex and straining a little, for he was a large dog, managed to lock the door behind them. She found that the best way to carry the dog was under her right arm with her left hand clasped around its underbelly. And this was how she got to the end of the street, half dragging, half lifting him.

It was a hot day and she was perspiring before she reached Princess Boulevard. She noticed a few people looking at her but, as she did not want to stop and explain, she walked past as steadily as she could manage. At the bus stop she put him down. His paws clicked against the white pavement and his shadow cast a lean dark stain behind him. He stood upright, supported entirely by rigor mortis. Behind them a queue began to form. As the first bus approached, Rose wanting to do the right thing stepped towards the platform.

'Excuse me,' she addressed herself to the conductor, 'but is it alright to bring a dog on the bus?'

''Course girl. As long as he behaves himself. Can't have dogs running up and down the . . .' His jaw dropped open as Rose heaved the rigid Rex up onto the platform. 'He's not too well,' he managed to say. 'There's something wrong with him.'

Rose was trying to fit him into place under the stairs usually reserved for bags and blocking the entrance by so doing. Behind her the queue was growing restless.

'Come on Missus . . .' Each one stopped as they got a proper look at the dog.

'You'll have to take him off,' the conductor said, while an elderly woman at the front of the bus began screaming.

'Rabies!' she yelled. 'The dog's stricken.' She pointed her walking stick towards the luggage compartment for emphasis. 'That's what they look like. I've seen it before, that look in their eye.'

'Hey Missus! Has yer dog got rabies?' said a young man behind Rose as he nimbly jumped back down from the platform.

'No, of course he hasn't,' Rose calmly explained with a smile. 'He's dead.'

'Dead!' squealed the old woman. 'The rabies has killed him!'

'Don't be soft mother,' a middle-aged woman sitting next to her said.

'For God's sake get it off,' someone requested.

'Is it contagious?'

'What? A dead dog?'

'Look Missus, you'll have to remove him. I can't have it

frightening the passengers,' and the conductor began to tug at the dog which had already become firmly wedged in the space.

He gave one desperate heave and the animal came free. Rose found herself swiftly escorted with her burden onto the pavement where she tottered, trying to regain her equilibrium, while holding Rex upright with his front paws on her shoulders like a partner at the Grafton Ballroom. His back legs began slipping away at the same time that Rose dropped her handbag. She foolishly bent down to try and retrieve it and the dog collapsed.

The bus driver, wondering what the delay was, glanced into his wing mirror in time to see a large dog slide on top of a woman and pin her to the ground.

'Good God!' he exclaimed inwardly, making a move to leave the cab and go to her assistance. But his attention was taken up with the sound of his mate banging against the glass. He wound up the leather blind and saw that the passengers were all out of their seats.

'Drive on for Christ's sake!' his mate mouthed to him, still banging on the glass in a state of extreme agitation.

'But that dog . . .' he shouted back, pointing to the street where Rose was lying.

'Never mind the bloody dog, I've just put it off the bus.'

'Is it vicious?' he breathed on the window.

'Vicious!' his friend repeated, looking shocked, 'vicious! It's lethal that's what it is. Drive on. Drive on.'

Behind the conductor he could see the gaggle of passengers, all talking at once and moving freely about in the aisle. Through the window he heard muffled words . . . 'Rabid', 'Dead', 'Mother of God, forgive us our trespasses . . .' for quite a few of them had started praying. 'It's mad, mad.'

Not sure who was afflicted he put his foot down hard on the accelerator.

The sergeant tapped his pencil on his notebook.

'Are you sure you saw the dog attack the woman?' he asked the busdriver. 'Why did you not go to her assistance?'

'It was ferocious, man, and I had a busload of passengers.'

'If it's true . . . and I'm not saying that I don't believe you,' he added quickly, 'it's just, well . . . a rabid dog is a rare thing in

England if that's what it was and I doubt very much . . .'

'I didn't say it was rabid, only mad and dangerous . . . and it's still . . . out . . . there . . .' The driver pointed a shaking hand to somewhere outside the door, his eyes popping from his head in wide-eyed terror.

'Have you got any witnesses?'

'Come outside mate.'

The sergeant followed him out into the station forecourt where, blocking off the entrance to the parking ground, as well as half of the pavement, was a green double-decker bus.

On Princess Boulevard, Rose was flagging down taxis. She had not had much luck. The first car to stop had driven off again immediately after the driver noticed, over Rose's shoulder, Rex fall sideways and lie rigid on the ground.

'Gerraway!' he said. 'I'm not taking that!'

The reaction of most of the cabs which stopped was similar if not always as vocal. The majority slowed down only to gather speed again without exchanging more than a horrified look.

'I'll pay Sunday rates,' she had offered one car in desperation, to be told that there were other passengers to consider.

'I can't let someone sit down where a minute before there's been a dead dog now can I?' one asked and Rose could not argue.

She stuck her thumb out in desperation at cars. She lugged the dog over to the traffic island at the end of the Boulevard. For if she stood on it she thought that she would have the chance of cars in both directions. She left Rex in the middle, lying on his side, while she ran back and forth from either end of the roundabout hailing passing vehicles. After half an hour she was exhausted. She leant against the pole of a traffic sign and drew her hand across her eyes wondering why life was so difficult. That moment she heard something pull into the lay-by at the park gates. Spinning round she saw that a lorry had stopped and two young people were clambering out from the passenger seat.

'Thanks Mate!' a lanky youth shouted up to the driver who was hidden from view as he helped a fair-haired girl down beside him. Two rucksacks were thrown from the great height of the cab and a voice shouted instructions for how to find the town centre.

Seizing her opportunity and her dog, Rose ran over the road.

'Excuse me, are you going in the direction of the city dump?' she shouted up. 'Or out past Walton?'

'Ay, alright,' said the voice. 'I'm turning off before that, but jump up, I'll take ye as far as Walton Hospital. Any good?'

Rose almost screamed with relief, but controlling herself began to explain. After all, she thought it was only fair to warn him.

'Look,' she began, 'I've got a dog.'

'Och that's alright, I like animals.'

'No, it's . . . you see . . . he's . . .' she stumbled over the words, her eyes beginning to fill with tears. 'I've had such a terrible time,' she sobbed. 'I . . . I . . .' words choked her, she began to cry. The driver's head appeared through the window. Peering down he saw Rose for the first time, standing weeping in her smart black suit and he thought there was something odd.

'Are you alright dear?' he asked, wondering whether to pull away.

'My dog's dead!' Rose burst out.

In a flash he was down on the pavement helping Rose up. He lifted Rex up and placed him gently beside her on the seat.

'Isn't it bloody awful,' he said indicating the dog, 'that anyone should be kept waiting that long.'

Eric came off his shift at eleven that morning. He took his time walking from where the factory bus dropped him off to his door, jangling his keys in his left hand. His right hand was free, for he carried no lunch box on Thursdays as he was home for his meal, which on any other Thursday he looked forward to and would hurry along. But today he strolled. He left his tools behind in his locker in the wash-up room, so he was empty handed. Like most nervous people who have difficulty placing their hands comfortably as they walk, Eric today showed his disquiet by the way he rattled his keys for something to do.

Outside the house he hesitated before mounting the step. Today, he thought, he would have to call his own bluff. Poor Rose. He knew that she was upset over Rex, but he also knew that the dog had to be got rid of.

In the hall he called out 'I'm home!' as he hung his donkey-jacket up on the peg. From the living room came the screeches from the cage as the two budgerigars fought over a piece of millet.

'Where's yer wellies?' one of them asked repeatedly.

'Rose?' he called into the empty kitchen. The cat was scratching against the door. He went through and drew back the bolt, opening it a crack and letting the sun from the back yard light up the dark flagstones on the floor.

'Come on then Snowy,' he said as a black cat walked knowingly into the kitchen and went straight to a dish on the floor.

'Who the hell are you?' he asked it, looking out into the yard for the other one. It began eating from the plate, and he laughed. 'So, you've come to Doctor Barnardo's too have you?' and he rubbed its ears.

'Rose!' he called again. She must be at the shops still, he thought. Then an idea struck him. If he hurried he could have the dog out and away before Rose was back. That would spare her some of the suffering. Yes, if he could act quickly now, he could just tell her that Rex was gone and maybe she would not have to see anything. He ran out to the phone box and dialled the police.

As the panda car cruised along Princess Park the car intercom began to crackle.

'Can you investigate a dog?' the message came through.

'Not another one!' the co-driver exclaimed, taking up the mouthpiece. 'But we've been everywhere looking for this mad one already. Hey! you don't think that it's the same dog do you?'

'Hardly,' the robotised voice answered. 'This one's dead. Bit of a problem disposing of the remains. If you could get round there and check it, then contact the salvage if you think it's necessary and get the bloke to fill in a form, O.K.?'

'Will do.'

Rose meanwhile had been let down with her cargo outside Walton Hospital where she struck lucky with a mini-cab driver who was coming away from the visitors' entrance intending to return to his depot.

'The sights I've seen girl,' he said indicating the hospital.

'When you've worked this stretch you get used to all sorts. Come on, let's try and get him in.'

Rex was slid inside through the open windows, where he lay with his front paws projecting from one side, his hind through the other. The only way that Rose could manage to hold him, so that he did not fall out, was to slide in underneath the dog and sit with it laying across her chest.

Poor Rex, she thought gazing up at him as he stared out the window. Tears began to prick at her eyes as the driver took off in the direction of the city dump.

The young constable waited in the hall as Eric gingerly unlocked the parlour door.

'Right,' he said authoritatively stepping in front of Eric into the room. 'Where is it?'

Eric followed behind and looked stupefied.

'It's not here,' he said sniffing the air cautiously. 'It's gone!'

The constable sighed and drew out his notebook.

'Is it a case of theft you want to report now?' he asked.

From the other side of the city Rose was making her way home by bus. She would probably be a little late with Eric's dinner. She wondered if he might like to go on a picnic instead? They could go to Princess Park and walk around Rex's old haunts. Her eyes suddenly felt warm and she knew that she would cry if she did not sit up and take control of herself quickly. She tried to console herself. After all, she thought, she had managed to see him off herself — and it had been a memorable end.

JAMES PLUNKETT

The Scoop

A discreet glance to right and left assured Murphy that no undesirable interest was being taken in his movements. He tilted his umbrella, turned expertly into the alleyway and entered the Poolebeg by the side door. He shook the January snow from his clothes before mounting the narrow stairs, and once inside the lounge called for the hot whiskey he had been promising himself all morning. He then looked around to see who was present.

There was the usual lunch break crowd; some actors from the nearby theatre, a producer, a sprinkling of civil servants who, like himself, worked in the nearby Ministry for Exports. His friend Casey was in deep conversation with a group which included three of the actors. There was a stranger among them, who seemed to be the focus of their attention.

Murphy's head was not in the best of health. He found the friendly buzz and the artificial brightness a relief after the drabness of the streets. He curled his fingers about his glass and sighed deeply. It was comfortably warm to the touch. As he lowered it from his lips his eye met Casey's and he nodded. Casey in return winked broadly. At first Murphy interpreted the wink as a wry reference to their mutual drinking bout of the previous evening, an acknowledgement of suffering shared. But Casey followed the wink by indicating the stranger with his thumb.

So that was it. The stranger had fallen into the clutches of the actors and there was some joke going on at his expense. Strangers who entered the Poolebeg had to run that risk. The actors were adept practical jokers who had given the other regulars many a memorable laugh at some casual's expense. They were good fellows, whose companionship Casey and Murphy relished. Murphy, eyeing the group with added interest, smiled with fellow feeling. In matters of this kind, he was one of the initiates.

He had called for his second whiskey and was wondering who the stranger could be, when Casey stood up and came across to him.

'What goes on?' Murphy asked.

'It's priceless,' Casey said in an undertone. 'Come on over and join us.'

'Who's his nibs?'

'An English journalist. Name of Smith.'

Murphy, preparing to relish the fun, asked, 'What's extraordinary about a journalist?'

'Do you know what he wants?' Casey said. 'A photograph of the IRA drilling and an interview with one of the leaders.'

'He doesn't want much, Murphy said, his eyes widening.

'Someone told him the Poolebeg was an IRA hangout. The actors are playing up to him. Come on over for God's sake. It's a gas.'

'Wait a minute,' Murphy said. 'I'll call another drink first.'

He did so. This was one of the things that distinguished the Poolebeg from other houses. There was colour and life in it, the regulars were a cut above the ordinary. One could discuss philosophy and religion with them. They knew what they were talking about. Or poetry. Or, if the mood prevailed, horse racing and dogs. And there was always the chance of some well-manoeuvred joke, the telling of which would enliven the dull hours in the office of the Ministry for Exports.

Murphy got his drink and followed Casey. He was introduced as Sean O'Murchu. The use of the Irish form of his name puzzled him but after a while he concluded that it must be part of the joke. The journalist took an immediate interest in him. He spoke of several recent raids on Northern Ireland by the illegal army and of the interest which his paper took in them. The editor wanted photographs and an interview. Since his arrival in Dublin he had been trying to make contact. Murphy hid his amusement behind an unsmiling mask. Then the journalist said:

'When I got the tip-off about this place I wasn't inclined to believe it, Mr O'Murchew. I don't easily despair, but I'd got several false leads already. But the moment I heard the Erse I knew you boys were straight.'

One of the actors affected a guilty start.

'We were speaking Irish and he overheard us,' he explained.

He said it directly to Murphy, in a tone of embarrassed apology, as though to forestall a possible reprimand.

'That's right,' another added. 'Mr Smith here took us completely by surprise.'

The first, fawning on Murphy, said:

'Oh — completely, sir.'

The word 'Sir' alarmed Murphy. He began to see what they were up to.

'What the hell do you mean by "Sir",' he demanded.

'Sorry — it slipped out,' the actor said. To Murphy's horrified eyes the actor appeared to blush.

He decided to take control of the situation at once. It was one thing to enjoy their leg-pull of an English journalist who was fool enough to think he could collect photographs of an illegal organisation such as the Irish Republican Army by walking into a public house and making a simple request. It was another thing if Murphy himself was to be pushed forward as an officer of that organisation and find God knows what dangerous reference to himself appearing in the English papers. Apart from the law, he was a civil servant and supposed to keep a mile clear of such things. It wouldn't do at all.

'Look here,' Murphy said, with a show of tolerance, 'I don't know what yarns these fellows have been spinning for you, Mr Smith, but I know nothing whatever about the IRA.'

'I appreciate your reticence, Mr O'Murchew,' the journalist assured him. 'Don't think I'd betray anything. Or that our paper is going to be unsympathetic. We know the wrongs of the Irish. We've carried articles on the Irish question that have rattled the Tories. That's why we want these pictures.'

'After all, think of the publicity,' one of the actors suggested.

'That's right. The organisation needs it,' said the other.

'A sympathetic review of *Aims*,' the first urged.

It took Murphy some time to collect his thoughts. The combined attack petrified him. The journalist, interpreting his silence for indecision, looked on hopefully.

'Look here,' Murphy said loudly, 'I know nothing about the bloody IRA. I'm a peaceable man with twenty years' service in the Ministry for Exports. I came here to have a quiet, contemplative drink . . .'

Casey suddenly gripped his sleeve.

'Keep your voice down, for God's sake.'

This Judas touch from his closest friend made Murphy almost shoot out of his chair.

'Are you going to side with them too. Holy God . . .'

'No, no, no,' Casey interrupted. 'Look who's just come in.'

Murphy looked up and immediately subsided.

A newcomer had taken his place at the counter and was ordering a drink with a grim inclination. He was tall, spare and hatchet-faced. He acknowledged those nearest him with a curt nod of the head and immediately excluded them again by studying his newspaper. Hempenstall was Murphy's immediate superior in the office. He seldom appeared in the Poolebeg. If he drank it was for a strict medicinal purpose. A sneeze in the course of the morning had caused him a moment of apprehension. Or a spasm of stomach cramp. Or a touch of 'flu. His world was essentially humourless and, since his wife's tragic death, a deliberately joyless one. His only release was the study of Regulations — all kinds of Regulations, which he applied rigorously. They were his only scruples. He spoke little, and that little only in the way of business.

'Do you think he heard?' Murphy asked in an undertone.

'If he didn't it wasn't *your* fault,' Casey answered sourly.

Hempenstall was Casey's superior too. The journalist leaned forward avidly. 'Who is he?'

'My superior,' Murphy whispered, using only the side of his mouth.

One of the actors said, 'The Wig'.

'I beg your pardon?'

'No one must know his real name,' the actor explained, 'so we call him The Wig.'

'Ah!' the journalist said, with complete understanding.

This was too much for Murphy. He tried to speak quietly, but emotion amplified what he had to say.

'Lookit here. This has got to stop. When I said it was my superior I meant my superior. I'm not going to sit here . . .'

Hempenstall was seen to lower his paper.

'Keep your goddam voice quiet,' Casey appealed. 'He's looking straight over.'

The journalist, who had formed his own conclusions, said:

'I suppose there's no use me making a direct approach to the . . . eh . . . Wig?'

The sudden change in Murphy's face gave him his answer. He added almost immediately: 'Sorry, Mr O'Murchew. I know how these things are. Forget it.'

He lowered his voice further and asked for what he termed a tip-off. A photograph of a contingent drilling would complete his assignment. It would be used in a manner which would reflect nothing but credit on a brave and resourceful organisation.

'You might as well tell him,' said one of the actors.

'He's a sympathiser. I've read his articles before.'

But the journalist was meticulous. It was the effect of four hot whiskies.

'Not a sympathiser — quite,' he corrected. 'My rule is — Understand one another first. Then judge. Present the case. I mean — fair hunt. What my colleagues and I are proud to call British Impartiality.'

'British Impartiality,' the actor approved, with the hearty air of being man enough to give the enemy his due.

Impulsively his colleague said, 'Shake.'

The journalist looked at the outstretched hand in surprise, then gripped it with genuine emotion.

'Now tell him,' the first actor said to Murphy.

Two matters troubled Murphy simultaneously. The first was the continuing presence of Hempenstall, who was uncomfortably within earshot. The second concerned the journalist and the actors. He found it impossible to decide which of them he would annihilate first — given the ability and the opportunity. He thought the journalist. He glanced around at the windows on his left and saw the snow dissolving in endless blobs against them. It tempted him with an idea for revenge. There was a mountain valley about seventeen miles distant, a lost, isolated spot which boasted a crossroads, a good fishing river and a public house. In summer Casey and he sometimes journeyed there by bus, for a little air and plenty of drink. In winter it was a godforsaken wilderness, frequently cut off from the outside world by deep drifts.

'Keep it very quiet,' Murphy whispered. They all leaned forward.

'There's a valley about seventeen miles out to the south, Slievefada,' he continued. 'Go there tomorrow and visit John Joe Flynn's public house.'

'How do I get there?' the journalist asked.

'Any of the car-hire firms will fix you up. Just tell them you want to go to Slievefada.'

'And what do I say to Flynn?'

One of the actors took over.

'When you walk in just say Dia Dhuit.'

'I get it — a password.'

This was better than the actor intended.

'Exactly. If Flynn answers Dia's Muire Dhuit, everything's O.K.'

'Do I mention Mr Murchew sent me?'

'No. If he asks you that, just say — The Mask.'

'The Mask.'

'Now you've got it.'

They spent some time teaching the journalist how to pronounce the simple Irish greeting which he had concluded to be a password and they wrote down the customary response phonetically so that he could study and recognise it. While they were talking Hempenstall left. Then the journalist found it was time to go too. His leave-taking was the occasion of a series of warm handshakes. As his bulk disappeared through the door, Casey felt the need of emotional release.

'Well . . . I declare to God,' he began. But having got that far, words failed him. He looked at the rest and they began to laugh,

the actors helplessly, Murphy uneasily. He was already apprehensive and inclined to regret his surrender to temptation.

His regret grew as the afternoon wore on. The office of the
Ministry for Exports was an oppressive warren of corridors and
offices, lit by hanging bulbs under ancient cowls. The whiskey
had left an unpleasant aftertaste. He felt depressed. Life, from
no tangible cause, bristled with vague but threatening uncer-
tainties. On afternoons such as this the thought often suggested
itself to Murphy that he was growing too old for the joking and
the drinking, a thought he now and then discussed with Casey.
They referred to the feeling mutually as a touch of Anno
Domini. Sometimes they wondered if it would have been better
to marry, even on the salary their modest abilities commanded.
There was troublesome correspondence on his desk too. A Lady
Blunton-Gough had started a campaign against the export of
live horses to France for use as food. She had founded a 'Save-
the-Horses' Committee. The trades unions had also made rep-
resentation to the Minister because the horses were being ex-
ported. Lady Blunton-Gough had publicly praised the humanity
of the working class. As it happened, prematurely. The trades
unions had soon made it clear that they had no objection to the
French getting their horse meat. They simply wanted to export
the meat in cans, in order to provide employment for the
butchering trade and the factory hands. As a result Lady Blunton-
Gough and the trades unions were now at daggers drawn. It
was part of Murphy's job to make a first draft of a letter to Lady
Blunton-Gough advising her that her representations were being
closely considered, and one to the Trade Union Congress to the
effect that in view of the heavy unemployment figures their
suggestion was receiving the sympathetic attention of the Minister.
Both organisations would publicise their respective replies. He
was struggling for the fifth successive afternoon with this un-
welcome problem when the buzzer indicated that he was wanted
in Hempenstall's office.

He found his superior sitting in an aroma of disinfectant,
sucking throat lozenges from a box on his desk.

'What I have to say is not official,' Hempenstall opened,
waving him to a chair.

Murphy made signs which conveyed that anything Mr Hempenstall cared to address to him would be avidly received.

'I speak in your own interest and that of the Department.'

'I understand, sir.'

'At lunch break today I visited the Poolebeg. I had a premonition of 'flu and felt the need of a preventative. You may have seen me?'

'Now that you mention it, I believe I did.'

'I happened to overhear a remark of yours, a reference to an illegal organisation. I have no doubt that it arose in the course of conversation . . .'

'I assure you it did.'

'Still, I think it my duty to remind you that even during his free time a civil servant remains a civil servant. Prudence requires him to avoid discussions of a political nature. Especially conversations involving the activities of an illegal army which operates in defiance of the Government he serves. I don't think I need labour the point. In mentioning it I have your career in mind. You are a long time with us.'

'Twenty years.'

'I thought even longer.'

'I'd like to explain that the subject of the IRA . . .'

'Quite. I trust it won't be necessary to refer to it again.'

'It arose, Mr Hempenstall . . .'

'Excellent. I won't keep you any longer from your desk.'

Frustrated and upset, Murphy returned to his desk. He found it more difficult than ever to concentrate on the question of horse meat. The evening dragged on; against the darkened windows he could sense the silent melting of snowflakes. After some nervous reflection he 'phoned Casey, who seemed to be in remarkably good form, and said to him:

'That was desperate carry on.'

'What was?'

'What-you-know.'

'Lord, yes. Priceless.'

'He seemed a bit of an ass.'

'Who?'

'Who-you-know.'

'It was good fun.'

'Do you think he'll really go?'
'Where?'
'Where-you-know.'
'It wouldn't surprise me.'
'Look. Meet me after the office.'
'The usual?'
'No. I think the other place.'
'Dammit. I can't. I've got an appointment.'
'That's a pity. Oh well. See you tomorrow. Lunchtime.'
'In the other place?'
'No. Better make it the usual.'
'Righto. By the way, I thought it very funny.'
'What?'
'Calling you The Mask.'
Murphy shuddered and replaced the phone.

Two days later nothing had happened and Murphy was beginning to see the bright side of the incident. The story of his
sending the journalist on a wild goose chase to Slievefada had
gone the rounds of the bars. In three different haunts he found
himself invited to give the story to the *habitués*. It was received
with tremendous hilarity. Here, their inner phantasies had been
translated into reality. A man with a camera, armed with a
harmless Irish greeting as a password, had gone off into the
snow-bound wilderness for a glimpse of the IRA. It was as
though Murphy had sent him hunting a Unicorn. Someone said
it was typical of the English and showed that they lacked
imagination. Another said it didn't. On the contrary, it showed
they had too much imagination. Somebody else said imagination
had nothing to do with it. It showed that the English had what
the Irish always lacked, faith in themselves. Another said not at
all; if it demonstrated anything it was that the English had faith
in the Irish. Murphy, when asked for his opinion, modestly
owned himself at a loss. It was dangerous to generalise. It was a
matter of judging the individual character he said, weighing him
up carefully and deciding how best to exploit his weak points.
Of course, it was all easier said than done.

'And you were the man to do it,' someone enthused. 'I take
off my hat to you.'

Then they all took off their hats to him, even those who were
not wearing them. Murphy found the experience pleasant. To
be well thought of in such company was the only taint of
ambition in his make-up.

Life had taught Murphy to believe in Fate. It had also taught
him not to trust it, a fact of which he was reminded the
following day when Hempenstall again called him to his office.

'You will remember our recent interview?' Hempenstall began.

'Of course, sir.'

'Have you seen the *Daily Echo*?'

'No, sir, I don't get the English dailies.'

'I have this morning's issue here. There is a photograph in it.'

Hempenstall unfolded a paper and laid it before Murphy who
bent down to examine it. His heart missed a beat. The photograph
showed about twelve men, spread out in wide formation, ad-
vancing up a snowy clearing which was flanked by pine trees.
The men were armed with rifles. The top caption read, *IRA
Manoeuvres*, and underneath, *Our Special Reporter scooped
this candid shot of warlike preparations in the Irish mountains*
(see below).

The accompanying article began:

*Within twelve hours of his arrival in Dublin, enquiries sent
our special reporter battling through snow and ice to a little
known village less than seventeen miles from the heart of the
Capital. The village — Slievefada, the mission . . .*

'Slievefada,' Murphy echoed involuntarily.

'You know the place?' Hempenstall said.

'Vaguely,' Murphy confessed.

'You are hardly being frank, Mr Murphy,' Hempenstall
accused. 'You spent your vacation there two years in succession.
We have it on your file. You will remember that during the
recent war the regulations required everyone of this staff to
furnish information as to his whereabouts when going on
leave.'

'Now I remember,' Murphy said. 'I was there for the fishing.
Funny I should forget.'

Hempenstall looked at him closely. He had the lowest possible
opinion of Murphy's intelligence, yet this new sample of its level
surprised him.

'I show you the photograph because you may feel I was over-severe the other day. I realise, of course, that your choice of Slievefada as a holiday resort and the present picture have no connection. But I trust it will help to drive home my point about careless talk in public places.'

'Very forcibly, sir.'

'These English reporters are everywhere. Think of your situation as a civil servant if one of them were to overhear you and approach you.'

'You make it very clear, sir.'

'Good. I want no action of any officer under my control to reflect discredit on my Section. You may go back to your desk.'

'Thank you, Mr Hempenstall.'

Murphy's appointment with Casey that evening was in none of their usual haunts. He was thankful for the darkness of the snowbound streets, thankful for the swarming tea-time crowds. He felt he might already be a hunted man. Now and again the picture flashed into his mind of a middle-aged body spreadeagled and lifeless among the shadows of some courtyard, the word 'Informer' pinned to its shabby coat. The body was his. Casey was already waiting for him in the restaurant. It was a cheap and noisy basement with a multi-colured juke box around which a group of teenagers wagged assorted bottoms. They drank two bowls of indescribable soup while Murphy urged the wisdom of going at once to Slievefada to question John Joe Flynn. Casey was disinclined.

'I don't see any sense in it,' he objected.

'Maybe you don't. But I do. It's the talk of every bar that I sent the reporter out there. If the IRA get to hear it God knows what will happen. They might even shoot me.'

'That's what I mean,' Casey said, making his point clearly. 'If we go to Slievefada they might shoot both of us.'

'John Joe's a friend of ours,' Murphy pleaded, 'he'll advise us for the best and let us know how we stand.'

'The roads are too bad,' Casey resisted, changing ground.

'There's no harm trying.'

'And look at the expense. Even if we persuade some driver to chance it, he's bound to charge us through the nose.'

'Not if we hire a self-drive.'

'And who'll drive it?'

'I will.'

'You,' Casey protested. 'Not bloody likely. I'd rather give myself up to the IRA and be done with it.'

'All right,' Murphy said at last, with a look of pitiable resignation. 'I'll go by myself.'

Two hours later Casey bitterly regretted the sense of loyalty which had made him yield to the unspoken challenge. He looked sideways at Murphy and wondered what strange love it was that induced him to stand by this thin, miserable, unprepossessing piece of humanity. He had a half bottle of whiskey in his lap which they had brought with them in case of emergency, but the potential comfort it contained failed to cheer him. The hired car slithered from ditch to ditch when they went downhill and slipped alarmingly when they climbed. Murphy crouched inexpertly over the wheel, his chin out, the rest of his face pinched and small with concentration and the cold.

'If I ever get back home alive,' Casey said finally, 'I'm going straight in to have myself certified.'

The car swung wildly but righted itself. Murphy's nerves were in a bad way. He snapped at him:

'There you go — distracting my attention.'

He crouched over the wheel once more. For some miles the headlights lit up a snowy wilderness. Soon it narrowed to a few yards. Slanting streamers of white surrounded and enclosed them. It was snowing again. The pine trees which marched up steep slopes on either side of the road disappeared. Once the near wheel slithered into the ditch and Casey got his shoes full of snow as he pushed and strained to lift it out. After less than a mile his feet were wet and cold. He stretched out his hand for the whiskey bottle. He began to grope about, calmly at first, then wildly.

'Holy God — it's gone,' he said at last.

'What's gone?'

'The whiskey.'

Murphy reacted automatically by pressing his foot on the brake. They careered from side to side, straightened, swung in a slow circle and, straightening once more, came to rest.

'How could it be gone?'

'It must have fallen when I got out to push you out of the ditch.'

'What'll we do?'

'What the hell *can* we do?'

'Nothing, I suppose. We'd never find it now.'

'You'd better drive on,' Casey said.

As they drove his feet got colder and colder. He no longer gave a damn about the IRA because he felt convinced he was going to die of pneumonia anyway. Once or twice he sneezed. After another half hour, during which they both thought more or less continuously of the whiskey bottle gradually disappearing under the falling snow, a view of the matter occurred to Murphy which he voiced for Casey's consolation.

'Ah well,' he said, 'thanks be to God it wasn't a full bottle.

At last they crossed the hump-backed bridge on the floor of the valley and swung left to the parking area in front of John Joe Flynn's. The two petrol pumps stood like snowmen, the blinds were down behind the windows, the door shut fast. John Joe could hardly believe his eyes. He dragged them in to the bar and over to the blazing log fire which reflected on the bronze and glass of the bar. Three or four times he repeated:

'Glory be to the Man Above Us, Mr Casey and Mr Murphy, well I declare to me daddy.'

But he wouldn't let them talk to him until he had poured out a welcome, which he brought over in two well-filled tumblers.

'Get that inside the pair of you now,' he said, 'and take off the shoes and stockings. Youse must be soaked to the bone.' He had a glass in his own hand too, which he raised.

'*Sláinte,*' he said.

'*Sláinte Mhór,*' they replied.

'You still keep a good drop,' Casey approved.

'Hold on there now,' John Joe said, 'till I get you something to go with it.'

He went down into the kitchen and they were alone for a while. Their shoes had left a trail of footprints on the flagged floor, their coats dripped wetly on the hanger. There was a smell

of groceries, of drink, of woodsmoke. The oil lamp slung from
the centre of the ceiling cast a yellow circle which was edged
with black. It made a faint buzzing noise which they found
comforting. John Joe returned with a pot of tea and a plate of
meat which they dispatched ravenously. They talked of the
weather, of mutual friends, of this and that. Then Murphy
pushed aside his empty plate and said, deliberately:

'We had a purpose in coming, John Joe.'

John Joe smiled and said:

'It occurred to me that it wasn't just to admire the scenery.'

They acknowledged the joke. Murphy took the *Daily Echo*
from his pocket and spread it on the table.

'As a matter of fact, John Joe, it was this.'

'The photograph,' he added, when John Joe looked puzzled.

John Joe put on his spectacles and studied the photograph
gravely. 'Well, I declare to me daddy,' he said at last, 'that fella
was in earnest, after all.'

'What fellow?' Murphy asked.

John Joe put his spectacles back in his pocket. They hindered
conversation.

'This fellow the other day. He blows in here from nowhere
with a bloody big camera and an English accent. He knew me
too. "Are you Mr John Joe Flynn?" says he. "That's what the
priest called me when he poured on the water anyway," says I,
"what's your pleasure?" He looked around once or twice as
though he felt someone might be listening. *"Dia Dhuit,"* says
he. *"Dia's Muire Dhuit,"* says I, surprised to hear an Englishman
using the Irish. The next thing was he leaned over and whispered
in me ear, "The Mowsk sent me."'

'The Mowsk?' Murphy echoed.

'I think that's what it was,' John Joe corrected, 'but I couldn't
be sure. You know the funny bloody way the English has of
talking. Anyway I left it at that and your man stayed the night.
The next morning after breakfast he told me he was here to get
a picture of the IRA drilling.'

'What did you say?'

'What would you say to that class of lunatic. I humoured
him. I told him it was a bloody serious thing to direct anyone to
IRA manoeuvres and asked for time to think it over.'

'What did he say to that?'

'What he said before. The Mowsk sent him. He had this Mowsk stuff on the brain. Anyway, half an hour later, just to get shut of him, I told him there might be something stirring if he went down to Fisher's Point at twelve o'clock or thereabouts. And for the love of God, says I to him, don't on any account let yourself be seen. Dammit, but I clean forgot about the boys.'

'The boys?' Casey repeated.

'An arrangement the boys had made here a few nights before.'

John Joe cocked his ear at the sound of a heavy engine which sent the windows rattling before it churned to a stop. 'This'll be Lar Holohan and his helper. Hold on for a minute.'

He went over to unlock the door and Murphy exchanged glances with Casey. Both had the feeling of being in the centre of a hotbed of illegal activity.

'He means "The Mask",' Casey whispered. It was quite unnecessary.

'I know,' Murphy answered. If anything, the whiskey had made his nerves worse.

The lorry driver and his helper sat down near them while John Joe got tea and bread and meat. It was a fierce night, the lorry driver told them, with a blizzard almost certain. When were they going back?

'Tonight,' Murphy said.

The lorry driver addressed his helper.

'They won't get back tonight, will they, Harmless?'

'Not unless they has an airyplane,' Harmless confirmed.

'We got ditched twice coming through the pass,' the lorry driver said, 'it's closed by now.'

'Will it be right in the morning?'

'With the class of a night that's in it now, I wouldn't think so. Not for two days at least.'

'Three,' Harmless corrected.

The food was brought and they attacked it with gusto. When they had finished, John Joe asked Murphy for the *Echo* and spread it in front of the lorry driver.

'Have a look at that, Lar,' he invited.

His eyes shone with expectation. Lar examined it thoroughly.

'Can you guess what it is?' John Joe asked after a while.

The lorry driver stroked his chin.

'It's not the IRA anyway,' he said at last. 'I recognise Tim Moore and John Feeney.'

'So do I,' Harmless added. 'I wouldn't accuse either of them of ambitions to shed their heart's blood for Ireland. Or anything else.'

'I'll tell you,' John Joe announced triumphantly, 'it's the dog hunt.'

The lorry driver guffawed.

'I declare to God,' he said, 'that's what it is.'

'Dog hunt?' Murphy said with a look of enquiry.

'You may remember Matt Kerrigan that lived by himself up the mountain,' John Joe began.

Murphy and Casey both remembered him, an old man who was something of a hermit.

'He died a few months ago,' John Joe said, 'but nothing would induce the bloody oul' mongrel he kept to quit the house.'

'A ferocious-looking blackguard of a brute it was too,' Harmless assured them. 'Not a Christian class of a dog at all.'

'That's not a word of a lie,' said the lorry driver.

'It stayed on at the house,' John Joe continued, 'and of course after a while it went wild.'

'It was never what you'd call tame,' Harmless said. He had a grievance against the dog which had once bitten him.

'It did terrible damage to poultry, and latterly it began to attack the sheep. So when the bad weather came and the boys got together to help bring the flocks down to the lower slopes they thought they'd kill two birds with the one stone and shoot the oul' dog if they could round him up as well. That's why they brought the guns.'

'They got it too,' Harmless said with relish, 'shot it above at Eagle Rock. They said it was mad as well as wild.'

'And that's the photograph the journalist got?' Casey asked.

'That's the photograph you see in front of you,' John Joe said. 'The boys setting off to get the bowler.'

'And he thought it was the IRA,' the lorry driver commented, looking at the photograph with renewed relish.

John Joe proceeded to tell the lorry driver why. He described the visit of the journalist and about sending him down to Fisher's Point to get shut of him. Three or four times the lorry driver nearly fell off his stool.

Murphy looked over at Casey. They found it impossible to join in the general laughter. Outside it was snowing hard. A wind had risen which made a deep, rumbling noise in the wide chimney. They thought of the pass filling moment by moment with its barrier of snow.

'We may as well have a drink anyway,' Murphy said; 'we'll have whiskey all round, John Joe.'

The lorry driver stopped laughing in order to hold up his hand and ask him to make his beer, explaining that he and his helper had had a skinful of whiskey already.

'It was when we were struggling with the lorry the second time we got ditched,' Harmless explained. 'Suddenly my foot kicked something. It was a half bottle of whiskey.'

'Someone must have let it fall,' said the driver.

'So we polished it off,' Harmless concluded and then cocked an ear to the night. He considered carefully.

'At least three days,' he added at last, meaning the Pass.

*

Harmless turned out to be right. Murphy and Casey stayed in John Joe Flynn's. There was nothing else they could do. They telephoned the post office and had a telegram sent on to Hempenstall, explaining that they were weather bound. On the same call John Joe sent a request to the post office to order a dozen copies of the *Daily Echo* and hold them. Everyone involved in the dog hunt would want one for himself, he said.

On the third day, while Murphy was gazing out of the window the thought occurred to him that the telegram they had sent to Hempenstall would bear the name of Slievefada Post Office as its point of origination. This was a fresh complication. It would be difficult to explain to Hempenstall. As he thought about it he grew pale. Even Casey noticed.

'What are you thinking about?' he asked.

Murphy's eyes dwelt in silence for a while on the snow-covered desolation outside. His pallor remained.

'Siberia,' he said eventually.

Follow On

The aim of all the activities in this section is to add to your enjoyment and understanding of the stories in this anthology. Some stories you may simply want to read and remember, others you may want to talk and write about, others may spark off memories and further ideas.

The suggestions for activities can be used to help you build up a folder for the coursework element of the General Certificate of Secondary Education. These activities fall into three broad areas:

> *Before reading* — enabling you to anticipate and speculate about what is going to happen.
>
> *During reading* — building up a picture of what is going on and what may happen next.
>
> *After reading* — allowing time to reflect on the setting, events, characters, issues and themes within the stories; giving opportunities for discussion, and for personal, critical and discursive writing.

Many of the activities will involve a mixture of individual, group and whole class work. You may not want to attempt all of the suggested activities but choose ones which particularly interest you. In some cases you may prefer to devise an activity of your own.

General Activities

> *Before reading*

▶ Read an extract, poem, play or short story which:
  — takes up similar themes or issues
  — presents characters/settings in similar/contrasting ways
  — is written in a similar/contrasting style or genre.

▶ Take some general issues or questions raised in the story and discuss them in advance. After reading the story, discuss how far your ideas and opinions may have changed.

▶ Use the titles and/or the first few paragraphs to speculate and predict what the story may be about.

▶ Take quotations from the story and speculate how it will develop.

During reading

▶ Stop at various points and review what has happened so far, then predict what might happen next or how the story may develop.

▶ Stop at various points and discuss why writers have made certain decisions and what alternatives were open to them.

▶ Decide who is telling or speaking the story.

▶ Look out for quotations that help reveal the meaning of the story.

▶ Make notes and observations on plot, character, relationships between characters, style and the way the narrative works.

▶ Consider the various issues, themes or questions relating to the story which you discussed before reading.

▶ Build up a visual picture of the setting in order to work out its significance in the story or to represent it as a diagram.

After reading

▶ Discuss a number of statements about the story and decide which best conveys what the story is about.

▶ Prepare a dramatic reading of parts of the text.

▶ Use the story as a stimulus for personal and imaginative writing:
— writing stories/plays/poems on a similar theme
— writing stories/plays/poems in a similar style, genre or with a similar structure.

▶ Discuss/write imaginative reconstructions or extensions of the text:
— rewriting the story from another character's point of view
— writing a scene which occurs before the story begins
— continuing beyond the end of the story
— writing an alternative ending
— changing the narrative from first to third-person and vice versa
— experimenting with style and form

— picking a point in the story where the action takes a turn in direction and rewriting the rest of the story in a different way.

▶ Represent some of the ideas, issues and themes in the story for a particular purpose and audience:
— enacting a public inquiry or tribunal
— conducting an interview for TV or radio
— writing a newspaper report or press release
— writing a letter to a specified person or organisation
— giving an eye-witness report.

▶ Select passages from the story for film or radio scripting; act out the rehearsed script for a live audience, audio or video taping.

▶ Write critically or discursively about the story, or compare one or more story, focusing on:
— the meaning of the title
— character, plot and structure
— style, tone, use of dialect, language
— build up of tension, use of climax, humour, pathos, etc.
— endings
— settings, themes and issues.

To Da-duh, In Memoriam

Before reading

▶ What memories do you have of someone in your family or a friend whom you no longer have contact with? Talk about these in groups.

▶ Having read Paule Marshall's introduction what kind of story do you expect 'To Da-duh, In Memoriam' to be?

During reading

▶ On one level this story is about a tussle to decide who and what is best. While you are reading, look out for the arguments and examples both sides use to try and win.
      After reading, discuss the examples you have found and what they tell you about the personality of the two characters involved.

▶ Make a note of the ways in which Paule Marshall evokes Barbadian life and life-styles. Look out for examples of Caribbean dialect.

▶ Watch for details which tell you that this is an autobiographical story.

▶ When the narrator sent her grandmother the postcard of the Empire State Building she probably wrote a few lines on the back (say 50—100 words). Bearing in mind her feelings on leaving Da-duh, imagine what she might have said. Compare what you have written with others in your group.

▶ Writing this story was of great importance to Paule Marshall, as she describes in its introduction; the title she chose suggests that it is an epitaph to Da-duh, she also says it has a wider meaning.

Write an appreciation of the story in which you concentrate on both the image she creates of her grandmother and on the wider associations the story as a whole holds for you.

As part of your writing consider the following:

— the author's use of contrasts and opposites to describe Da-duh.
— the pride her grandmother has in Barbados and the way the narrator slowly undermines it.
— the sense of regret and emptiness the narrator has in her hollow victory.
— the similarities she sees between herself and her grandmother.
— the ending of the story.
— wider issues such as the rivalry between youth and age, the undermining of one culture by another, the importance of understanding and valuing different lifestyles.

▶ *Either:* Rewrite this story as a script for a radio or television play, bringing out the strength of the dialogue.

Or: Imagine you are making a film profile of Da-duh and Barbados for a New York audience. Which aspects of her life will you choose to focus on? Write the outline for your documentary detailing which scenes and words you will include. This task is probably best done in pairs or small groups.

▶ Look again at the section which begins 'Over the weeks I told her about . . .' and ends with 'the world's changing up so I can scarce recognise it anymore' (pages 13—14).

Imagine you had to explain the way you live and the things you do to somebody who lives in a very different way, remembering you may have to describe all sorts of things you take for granted.

Write the conversation you have. Rehearse, then tape it.

▶ Imagine you are trying to explain about the latest dance or fashion, or the current songs you like, or the magazines and comics you enjoy reading, to an older person who didn't have or do anything like that when they were young. Write and act out the scene.

Chemistry

Before reading

▶ This story brings together three generations. What particular sources of conflict might exist between the members of the family? Discuss in groups what types of incident cause tension or conflict in your family.

During reading

▶ Read the first section of the story down to the words, 'as if she had seen something appalling' (page 18). In pairs:
  — discuss what themes and issues are raised in this section.
  — pick out three or four phrases or sentences which seem particularly important.

▶ Stop reading after the words ' "Darling. Please, I'll explain. Darling, darling" ' (page 26). *Either* in pairs discuss how you think the story will end *or* write your own ending to the story.

▶ Look out for lines which create a feeling of mystery and suspense in the story. For example: 'But if I really believed Father was gone for ever — I was wrong' (page 19).

▶ Look out for any references to 'laurel'. Laurels are normally kinds of glossy-leaved shrubs or bushes.

▶ Note any references to age, time and seasons, so you can work out how many years the narrative covers.

After reading

▶ Using the lines 'Chemistry is the science of change. You don't make things in chemistry — you change them. Anything can change' as a title, write a critical appreciation of the story as a whole. As part of your writing think about the following points:
  — the opening and closing sections of the tale.
  — the changing relationships between Ralph and the narrator's mother, Ralph and the grandfather, the grandfather and the mother.
  — the themes of death and loneliness.
  — the title.
  — the meaning and significance of the above lines in the story.

▶ Recast the narrative from *either* Ralph's *or* the mother's viewpoint.

▶ Imagine you are the police officer in charge of investigating the death. Write your report on the causes and motive based on interviews with the main characters and on other evidence you found in the house and in the grandfather's shed.

Your report could include notes and quotes taken during interviews, jottings about material you think is important, and a concluding summary in which you draw together threads from the information you have found.

▶ After grandfather's death the narrator discovers a collection of tapes on which are recorded the old man's diaries covering the period of the story. Reconstruct these taped-diaries.

▶ Imagine that as he grows up, the boy decides to write a letter to his own son to tell him about his great-grandfather.

Write this letter, using the story to build up a vivid picture of the grandfather's character.

▶ In pairs discuss some of the important incidents and experiences of your own childhood and write a story built round such memories.

Your story can be true or made up, or a mixture of the two. If you wish you could structure it in the same way as Graham Swift by writing it in sections which deal with separate recollections and which build together to form a whole. You could also use flashbacks to set the scene and illuminate what follows.

The Custodian

Before reading

▶ What does the title of this story indicate it may be about?

▶ Read the first paragraph of the story and predict how you think the story will develop. Also consider what the author hoped to achieve by starting the story in this way.

During reading

▶ Look out for the things which cause the old man to fear and worry.

▶ Look out for the appearance of the buzzard about half-way through the story.

▶ Make a note for your own writing how Susan Hill evokes scenes through the technique of appealing to our senses. Look at her detailed descriptions of the natural world.

▶ Notice how she builds up tension to the point where there is the sighting of 'a man with a gun under his arm' (page 38).

▶ Stop reading at the break in the text on page 40. In groups, predict how the story could develop now the boy's father has arrived.

Stop reading after the words, 'He did nothing. He knew' (page 51). Predict how you think the story will end.

After reading

▶ This story could have ended with the sentence 'Winter came' (page 52). First consider how an ending like this would have affected the story as a whole and your reaction to it. Then consider how the last five lines lead to a different interpretation. For example:
— What do they indicate about the character of the boy and about his relationship with his father *and* the old man?
— Do they suggest a further reason why the author chose to call the story 'The Custodian'?
Would you have preferred a different ending?

▶ The rural setting of 'The Custodian' is carefully evoked by Susan Hill, especially in the first half of the story, and it links directly with the feelings and security of the old man and the boy. For example:
— the story begins at the end of winter, looking forward to spring, but ends with the coming of winter.
— many of the boy's early experiences are associated with going for walks in the countryside.
— the shooting of ducks and the appearance of a buzzard occur directly before the appearance of Gilbert Blaydon.
Referring closely to the text, illustrate the ways in which this is done and suggest reasons why this emphasis changes in the second half of the story after Blaydon comes to stay.

▶ Write a second instalment to this story which either begins or ends with the last five lines of Susan Hill's original and which deals with the lives of the boy and his father in the months since they left the old man. Think about the following before you begin:
— how the father persuaded his son to come with him (did he finally tell him he was his father? did he talk about why he had left him as a baby and what he had done since? did he talk about the boy's mother?).
— what the boy made of life in the town.
— if he ever thought of the old man (did he ever want to see him again or had he forgotten him?).

▶ Bringing up a child, especially on your own, can present many problems but also give many rewards. This story emphasises the fears and anxieties of the old man and some of the problems he had to overcome because he was a man on his own.

Write an essay in which you consider the problems and rewards of bringing up a child on your own, giving both equal consideration.

Comparisons: To Da-duh, In Memoriam, Chemistry, The Custodian

▶ These three stories are all about relationships between young and old. Each raises important questions about such relationships and deals with them in similar and contrasting ways.

In pairs, using a chart like the one below, note down points which strike you as important in each story, adding more categories if necessary. (A few have been given to start you off.)

CATEGORIES	*To Da-duh*	*Chemistry*	*Custodian*
Place/setting	v. impt. eg . . .	Grandfather's shed impt.	
Age/relationship of main characters			7/71. Are man & boy related?
Family setting			
Outsiders			
Beginnings/ endings		begins and ends with same memory	
Narrative style	first-person		
Time			
Autobiographical/ fictional			
Issues raised			
Lessons learnt, etc.			

Compare your charts with others in the group. Now write an essay in which you compare the three stories, using some of the categories from the chart together with quotations from the texts.

The Gun

Before reading

▶ This story is set in South Africa. Before you begin reading talk about what you know of the apartheid regime of government and the social and political conditions it imposes on black people.

During reading

▶ Look out for examples which illustrate the repression of the apartheid regime, its effects on black people and their resistance against it.

▶ Note down details of setting and the ways in which the author develops the plot and sustains suspense.

▶ Look out for references to the gun which illustrate its central importance to the story.

▶ Stop reading after the words, 'The safety catch came undone! . . . help me tie something around . . .' (page 64). In pairs, predict how you think the story will end. Remember to base your predictions on what has happened in the story so far.

▶ Some words in this story may be unfamiliar to you. Here is a short glossary:
pap — a porridge made from corn
jong — boy
donder — thrash

After reading

▶ During the story Esi has a number of experiences which directly affect the decision he takes at the end. For example:
— the story of the leopard's attack on the enclosure.
— the attitude the people of Mapoteng have to his father.
— the soldiers' raid on his aunt's house.
— growing rumours about the activities of the 'MKs'.
— the arrival of Williams and the way he treats the family.
  Linked to each of these is the symbol of the gun and the power it holds for those who possess it.
  Write an essay which illustrates Esi's growing understanding of the society in which he lives and which explains why he took the actions he did.

▶ It is essentially through an accident that Esi is propelled in the end into a position where he has to take action against the State. What might have been his course had this particular accident not taken place? Was confrontation eventually inevitable? Talk about this in pairs, then in larger groups.

▶ What impressions do you have of:
(a) Mackay   (b) Hendriks   (c) Williams?
   What do you think motivates them and informs their opinions? What would their verdict be on Esi's actions at the end of the story? Write up your ideas as a series of short interviews, then tape them with a partner.

▶ Retell — either in written or oral form — 'The Gun' from Esi's point of view. Remember to use the first-person narration. When others in your group have read or listened to your version, ask them to compare it with the original third-person narrative.

▶ Imagine you are an investigative journalist assigned to make contact with the 'MKs' and report on their activities and aims. You have met and interviewed a number of the freedom fighters including Esi; you have also interviewed Esi's father and Williams.
   Write up your findings as a feature article for a British newspaper.

▶ Imagine that Esi and his father meet up two years later. Write up the conversation they might have, in which each argues why he has chosen to live the way he does. Act out their encounter.

▶ Write an essay about the apartheid system in which you:
   — explain its historical and political development and any changes which have been introduced in recent years.
   — outline the current situation in South Africa.
   — give your own views on apartheid and its future.
   You will need to do some research for this assignment, looking in history books, newspapers and perhaps at the works of other writers about South Africa — e.g. Nadine Gordimer. Beverley Naidoo's own essay on pages 66—7 will be especially valuable.

The Tunnel

Before reading

▶ What does the title suggest the story may be about? Think carefully about the different meanings and associations it could have. In pairs, make a list of the things it suggests to you and compare them with your group so that a collective list can be drawn up.

▶ In pairs or small groups, draw up a skeleton outline of a typical 'runaway-young-love' story.

What ingredients do these stories generally have?

How do they usually begin, develop, end?

On what do you base your ideas: other well-known stories? books and magazines you read? TV?

During reading

▶ Look out for the clues in the story which help you decide the approximate date it took place.

▶ Make a note of the various artists and writers referred to — find out who they were.

▶ Look out for reasons the author may have had for calling this story 'The Tunnel' and for ideas for other possible titles.

▶ Note down any ways in which the story conforms to a typical 'runaway-young-love' tale and the ways in which it differs.

▶ Stop reading after the words, 'Then things changed' (page 77). Predict any possible changes in their lifestyle from this point on.

After reading

▶ Re-read the section of the story which describes the boys digging the tunnel. It begins, 'But they didn't go. They re-appeared the next morning' (page 87).

Either: Re-write this incident in the form of a poem, using words and ideas of your own or taking phrases and sentences from the story and adapting them.

Or: Write a report for the local paper covering what the boys did to the local school and the tunnel they dug. You could include interviews with local residents, the school caretaker, council workers and so on, who may have seen some of what went on and have views to express on what is happening to the area in general.

▶ In groups, discuss the reasons the author may have had for calling this story 'The Tunnel', both the obvious and the not so obvious. Also think of alternative titles he could have chosen; here are some to think about:

The Spring and Summer of . . .   Romeo and Juliet
Clancy's Uncle   A Bed by the Window
Runaways

Decide on the title you think best suits the story and write about your reasons for choosing it (with quotations from the text) and for discounting some of the others you thought of.

▶ In some ways this story follows the accepted pattern of traditional 'runaway-young-love' stories, but certain events and situations described in the story break away from this pattern.

Using the skeleton outline you made before reading, go back and read the story again making notes of the usual and unusual elements within the story. A chart like the one below may help you to organise your notes.

EVENT/EXAMPLE	*Usual*	*Unusual*
Different backgrounds		
Poor boy/rich girl		
Parents' attitude		
How they met, etc.		

Using your notes write an appreciation of the story. Here are some points for you to consider:
— Would things have been different if the narrator was from a posh background and Clancy from a poor background?
— Why were events like the narrator's scalding his hands and the boys digging the tunnel described in so much detail?
— Why did the author end the story in the way he did? Is this the usual ending for a love story?
— What did you like/dislike about the story?
— Did it seem realistic?

▶ Rewrite 'The Tunnel' as a series of entries in Clancy's diary. Remember to use the first-person 'I' narrator from Clancy's point of view and only include events in the story which she was present at.

▶ 'I nearly always write in the first person, partly because I prefer the located, ground-level view this gives, but partly because the narrator is every bit as important to me as the narrative' (page 92).

Discuss this comment of the author's with reference to 'The Tunnel'. In what ways does Graham Swift's essay contribute to your appreciation of this short story?

Lunch Hour Rush

Before reading

▶ 'Lunch Hour Rush' is about a café waitress called Milly and describes a typical rush-hour in her day when she has to keep her mind *on* her job and *off* things which may be troubling her outside work.

In pairs, make a list of the things a waitress would have to do and cope with during one of the busiest parts of her day. Also consider the employment conditions of restaurant/café workers such as: pay, hours, security, perks, holidays, customer expectations and so on.

During reading

▶ Apart from all the one-off customers who use the café at lunchtime, Milly has certain regulars. They are:

Ham-and-Eggs   The Usual   Two typists
Her late customers   Five young lawyers

While you are reading look out for the way they treat her and the ways in which she responds to them.

▶ Note down details of Milly's life outside work and the way these affect her mood throughout the story.

▶ Stop reading after the words, 'It brought the boss himself from his office' (page 101). Predict how the story will end.

After reading

▶ Roger Mais chose to write this story in the third person, almost as if he were one of Milly's regulars, perhaps even her late customer who has just had his book published. By doing this he can mix both the lighthearted and the more serious aspects of the story.

Comment on the way he has decided to write and structure the story and how the story would have changed if it were written as a first person narrative through Milly's eyes.

▶ Imagine that job advertisements have to describe in detail *all* aspects of the job. Write a description of Milly's job which covers: pay, hours, job security, holidays, 'perks', appearance, customer expectations, ability to carry heavy loads, putting up with the constant heat and smell of food, who's to blame when things get broken, etc.

In your advert try to inject some humour by choosing language which deliberately exaggerates some aspects of the job and plays down others so as to give a better impression of what it's really like. For example:
— 'would suit someone with few outside interests'.
— 'a good opportunity to practise the skill of hiding your real feelings'.
— 'wearing protective clothing is recommended for more than one reason'.

▶ Imagine each of the regular customers were asked to say why they went to the café for their lunch, and to describe what happened in the café the day the story takes place. What would they say? Write down their comments as a series of quotes, or, in groups, act as interviewer and customers and role play their comments.

▶ Write a story or play of your own set during a lunch hour, perhaps in another setting such as a school or factory, using a similar style and structure to Roger Mais's.

An Affair Of The Heart

Before reading

▶ In small groups try to remember some of the people you knew when you were very young.
What sort of games did you play? How real did they seem to you at the time?
Did you ever imagine living in a special place completely different from where you actually lived? What sort of place was it?
Did certain things worry or frighten you because you didn't quite understand what they were or how they worked?

During reading

▶ Look out for words which help identify where the story is set.

▶ Some words may be unfamiliar to you. Here is a short glossary:
pipis — a kind of shell-fish
bach — holiday cottage
kauri — a tree from which gum is collected
kumaras — sweet potatoes
cobbers — friends, mates

▶ Stop reading after the words, 'It's my belief that only the very toughest sort of people should ever go back to places where they've been happy' (page 107).

In pairs, discuss how you think the rest of the story will develop.
— Will the Crawleys' bach still be on the beach?
— What will it be like?
— What age will Mrs Crawley and her children be?
— What will have become of them?

Remember that earlier in the narrative we are told that Joe is Mrs Crawley's favourite and that she didn't really notice the girls. Also, that the narrator had a feeling 'that going mad over a person in that way could turn out to be quite a terrible thing' (page 106).

| *After reading* |

▶ Near the beginning of the story the author writes: 'I haven't set out to philosophise. I've set out to tell you about a woman who lived in a bach not far beyond that bay of ours, and who, an old woman now, lives there to this day' (page 103).

Just over half-way through he writes: 'It's my belief that only the very toughest sort of people should ever go back to places where they've been happy' (page 107).

And he concludes with the words: 'But I never understood until last Christmas day . . . how anything in the world that was such a terrible thing, could at the same time be so beautiful' (page 109).

Bearing in mind these quotations write an appreciation of 'An Affair Of The Heart' in which you discuss:
— how far this story is only about Mrs Crawley, an old woman living on a beach.
— the effect these childhood experiences had on the narrator's life.
— what is meant by the closing lines of the story.
— why the author chose his title.

▶ This story is written as a first person narrative and so all the characters and events are seen through the narrator's eyes. It is largely a descriptive story with little dialogue. Rewrite the following sections as a third person narrative so that the reader learns more about each of the characters involved. Introduce more dialogue if necessary.

(a) The section which begins 'Well, we went over to look' and ends 'there was something in what mother said that made us feel a little frightened' (pages 103—4).

(b) The section which begins 'He told me all he knew' and ends 'she always explained that she was buying it for Joe' (page 109).

▶ Write your own account of an incident or a series of events which might have led to Mrs Crawley being deserted by her son and daughters.

▶ Write a story of your own about an event which took place a long time ago and which has made a lasting impression on you.

▶ Imagine that as an adult you revisit a person or a place you have not seen for a long time. How do you think your childhood memories would change with a second look? Write a story or a sequence of poems about what happens.

Memento Mori

Before reading

▶ Translated from the Latin this title means 'Memorable End'. It is a story about the difficulties a pet owner has in getting her dead dog buried. You may think this is a sad subject for a story — in fact it's very funny. The thing to remember is that Rex, the dog, had a very happy and contented life and died peacefully at a ripe old age!
   The main ingredients of the story are:
   — a rather large dead dog.
   — a dustbin strike.
   — a devoted owner, who is an incurable animal lover.
   — her husband, who is sympathetic but wants his wife to be more realistic.
   — a local dump which is on the other side of town.
   In pairs, predict how you think the story could go!

During reading

▶ Look out for words and phrases which illustrate the relationship between Rose and Eric. For example: 'the timed response', 'always on cue', 'Eric had always been fearfully proud of Rose'.

▶ Make a note of the people Rose encounters.

After reading

▶ Moy McCrory manages to turn an unhappy event into a very amusing story. Using examples from the text show how the language she uses and her turn of phrase manage to create this humorous effect.

▶ Imagine that, as well as phone calls to the police station, a number of calls have been made to the local paper informing on various stages of Rose's journey across town. You are the reporter assigned to get the facts. Write an article about what happens while you are trying to complete this task and which finishes with the report you eventually decide to write. Think up an eye-catching headline for your article.

▶ Act out the tales that are told by one or more of the people who come into contact with Rose during 'Memento Mori' when they get home that evening. For example:
— the desk officer at Granby police station.
— the bus conductor.
— the bus driver.
— the lorry driver.
— the mini-cab driver.

▶ Turn this story into a script for a radio or television play. If you are writing for radio remember that *sound* effects are important; if writing for television, plot out the various *visual* scenes you will need.

▶ Continue the story from where Moy McCrory leaves things, and write about what happens when Rose returns home. As far as possible write in the style of the original. Then try a dramatised reading of your piece.

▶ Look again at the telephone conversation Rose has with the desk officer and use it as the basis for your own piece of writing about a misunderstanding between two people on the phone. It will help if you plan this writing in pairs by role-playing the misunderstanding first. Tape your finished product.

The Scoop

| Before reading |

▶ This story is set in the south of Ireland and refers to the Irish Republican Army (IRA). Before you begin reading make sure you understand the role played by this organisation in Ireland.

▶ What does the title of the story suggest it may be about? Which organisations are normally involved in getting 'Scoops'? How do they get them? Are they always what they seem?

▶ This story is full of humour, mainly at the expense of an English journalist (beware of believing anything which is said to him!). However, the repercussions of the way this journalist is 'set-up' affect some of the other characters as well. Look out for the points in the narrative when the characters are caught out by the joke they played. Make a list of them.

▶ Note down features of language which help identify the story's setting.

▶ Look out for descriptions of Murphy and Casey, their likes, dislikes, jobs, ages, personalities and so on.

After reading

▶ In groups re-write in the form of a play the section which begins ' "When I got the tip-off about this place . . ." ' (page 123) and ends 'His leave-taking was the occasion of a series of warm handshakes' (page 126).

You may wish to change some of the existing dialogue and add to it. You will also need to incorporate the speakers' actions and tones of voice into stage directions. Act it out.

▶ Write the scene which takes place between Murphy and Hempenstall when Murphy finally returns to work after the story ends. To refresh your memory of previous conversations they have had, look again at pages 127—8 and 130—1.

▶ Write the newspaper article which could appear in an Irish Daily when the *truth* about what happened at Slievefada emerges.

▶ Reread the telephone conversation between Murphy and Casey on pages 128—9. Write and act out a conversation between you and a close friend which is in a similar style; in other words, so that an eavesdropper would have little idea what was going on!

▶ Write a story of your own in which a practical joke turns out to involve more than was at first expected.

▶ Taking 'Memento Mori' and 'Scoop' together talk about what makes them funny stories. How are the plots constructed? What phrases and vocabulary make you laugh? Do they share common ideas and approaches to comic writing? Compare the two tales with other comic writing that you have enjoyed. Can you identify certain ingredients that you might borrow for your own writing?

Further ideas for group and individual work

▶ As well as telling a story, writers often want to make us think deeply about an idea or theme or issue. Make a list of the various themes raised in this collection. Which themes do the stories have in common? Have any of the stories made you rethink your opinions or beliefs?

▶ Which characters in the stories did you enjoy reading about or even identify with? Write your own story centering on one of these characters, or bring together characters from different stories.

▶ What are your reactions to the ways in which the stories end? Look closely at the concluding lines of each story. If you find the ending unsatisfactory, try rewriting — or acting out — an alternative one.

▶ 'The Tunnel' uses the first-person 'I' narrator to tell the story, while 'The Scoop' has a third-person narrator observing the action from outside.
   What seem to you the advantages and disadvantages of the different types of narrative standpoint? (Graham Swift's essay on pages 91—2 makes some illuminating comments on this subject.) Rewrite any of the stories, changing the narrator's point of view.

▶ When people write fiction they often do so based on something they have seen or done themselves. Which of these stories seem to you in any way autobiographical? What clues do you look for?

▶ Why does someone behave in the way they do? What causes them to take one line of action rather than another? What motivates the characters in these stories? Working in groups, choose one of the stories. Then take it in turns to play the part of one of the characters. Each character is placed in the witness-box and quizzed by the others as to why they behaved as they did in the story. You might start with 'The Gun' or 'Chemistry'.

▶ Many of the stories in this collection focus on what Paule Marshall identifies as 'the basic theme of youth and old age to suggest rivalries'. Looking back through the volume discuss how *you* might have reacted had you been caught up in these rivalries. Where do your sympathies lie in the stories?

▶ How important a role do *memories* play in any of the stories? Write up your conclusions.

▶ Mount a dramatised reading — complete with sound effects and music — of one of the stories. This is best practised in small groups and then presented to a larger audience.

▶ 'A first reading makes you want to know what will happen; a second makes you understand why it happens; a third makes you think'. How true is this in your reading and re-reading of the stories in *That'll Be The Day*?

▶ 'What so many short stories have in common is that they are saying, in one form or another: "Isn't it strange?" They are reminding us that life, even everyday life, is more peculiar, more mysterious than we often assume' (page 91).

'Stories exist to entertain and excite, but they are also a process of recovery, in both senses of the word — they have a therapeutic power' (page 92).

Using these comments from Graham Swift as starting points, write a critical appreciation of any three stories in the collection.

Further Reading

To Da-duh, In Memoriam by **Paule Marshall** is taken from her collection *Merle and Other Stories*. Students are also recommended to read *Brown Girl, Brownstones* and *Praisesong of the Widow* (all published by Virago) by the author.

Related reading:

The Bluest Eye, Toni Morrison, Panther (1981)
Black Lives, White Worlds, Keith Ajegbo (ed.), Cambridge University Press (1982)
Gather Together In My Name, Maya Angelou, Virago (1985)
Poona Company, Farrukh Dhondy, Gollancz (1980)
Roots, Alex Haley, Picador (1978)
Green Days by the River, Michael Anthony, Heinemann (1973)
In The Castle of my Skin, George Lamming, Longman (1979)
Going To Meet The Man, James Baldwin, Corgi (1967)
Lesley's Life, Lesley Davies, Longman Knockouts (1986)

Chemistry by **Graham Swift** is taken from his collection *Learning to Swim and other Stories* (Picador). His novel *Waterland* is also recommended reading.

Related reading:

The Fox in Winter, John Branfield, Collins Cascades (1983)
The Old Man and the Sea, Ernest Hemingway, Panther (1976)
The Cay, Theodore Taylor, Puffin (1973)
Roll Of Thunder, Hear My Cry, Mildred Taylor, Puffin (1980)

The Custodian by **Susan Hill** is taken from her collection *A Bit of Singing And Dancing*. Students may also enjoy her novels *I'm The King of the Castle* and *Strange Meeting*, (all published by Penguin).
Related reading:

Cider With Rosie, Laurie Lee, Longman Imprint (1976)
A Hoxton Childhood, A. S. Jasper, Centerprise (1972)
The African Child, Camara Laye, Fontana (1959)
Old Mali and the Boy, D. Sherman, Penguin (1968)
The Pigman, Paul Zindel, Armada Books (1976)
Summer's End, Archie Hill, Wheaton (1976)
My Oedipus Complex, Frank O'Connor, Penguin (1984)
The Open Road, Jennifer Gubb, Onlywomen Press (1984)

The Gun by **Beverley Naidoo** is previously unpublished and was specially written for this anthology. Students are also recommended to read her short novel *Journey to Jo'burg* (Longman Knockouts).
Related reading:

Things Fall Apart, Chinua Achebe, Heinemann (1962)
Selected Stories, Nadine Gordimer, Penguin (1983)
To Kill A Mockingbird, Harper Lee, Pan (1974)
Bandiet: Seven Years in a South African Prison, Hugh Lewin, Heinemann (1982)
The Grass is Singing, Doris Lessing, Panther (1980)
Violence, Festus Iyayi, Longman Drumbeat (1979)
Cry the Beloved Country, Alan Paton, Penguin (1970)
Absolute Beginners, Colin MacInnes, Alison & Busby (1980)
Talking In Whispers, James Watson, Fontana (1985)

The Tunnel by **Graham Swift** is, like 'Chemistry', taken from his excellent collection *Learning to Swim and Other Stories* (Picador).
Related reading:

See You Thursday, Jean Ure, Puffin (1981)
Your Friend, Rebecca, Linda Hoy, Bodley Head (1981)
19 Is Too Young To Die, Gunnel Beckman, Macmillan (1971)
A Comprehensive Education, Roger Mills, Centerprise (1979)
The L-Shaped Room, Lynne Reid Banks, Longman Imprint (1976)
The Catcher in the Rye, J. D. Salinger, Penguin (1969)
It's My Life, Robert Leeson, Armada Lions (1981)
Sumitra's Story, Rukshana Smith, Bodley Head (1982)
My Darling, My Hamburger, Paul Zindel, Armada Books (1978)
Johnny Jarvis, Nigel Williams, Puffin (1983)
Gregory's Girl, in *Act Now* series, Cambridge Univ. Press (1983)

An Affair of the Heart by **Frank Sargeson** comes from a collection titled *The Stories of Frank Sargeson* (Penguin).
Related reading:

A Kind of Loving, Stan Barstow, Corgi (1983)
The Go-Between, L. P. Hartley, Penguin (1970)
Daughters of Passion, Julia O'Faolain, Penguin (1982)
The Lonely Londoners, Samuel Selvon, Longman Drumbeat (1979)
The Stories of Ronald Blythe, Chatto & Windus (1985)
Separate Tracks, Jane Rogers, Fontana (1984)

Lunch Hour Rush by **Roger Mais** is from his *Collected Short Stories* (Longman).
Related reading:

Portraits, Kate Chopin, The Women's Press (1979)
The Charlotte Perkins Gilman Reader, The Women's Press (1981)
Best West Indian Stories, Kenneth Ramchand, Nelson (1982)
A Flag On The Island, V. S. Naipaul, Penguin (1969)
Ways of Sunlight, Samuel Selvon, Longman Drumbeat (1979)
You Can't Keep A Good Woman Down, Alice Walker, The Women's Press (1982)
West Indian Stories, John Wickham (ed.), Ward Lock (1981)
Gorilla, My Love, Toni Cade Bambara, The Women's Press (1984)
Stories of the Waterfront, John Morrison, Penguin (1984)

Memento Mori by **Moy McCrory** is taken from her fine collection titled *The Water's Edge* (Sheba Feminist Publishers).
Related reading:

Women's Part. An Anthology of short fiction by and about Irishwomen 1890–1960, Janet Madden Simpson, Arlen House (1984)
The Female Line. Northern Irish Women Writers, Ruther Hooley (ed.), Universities Press (1985)
Short Stories from Ireland, Kenyon Calthrop (ed.), Wheaton (1979)
The Secret Self: Short Stories By Women, Hermione Lee (ed.), Dent (1985)
The Stories of John Cheever, Penguin (1982)
Young Adolf, Beryl Bainbridge, Fontana (1979)
Lucky Jim, Kingsley Amis, Penguin (1970)
Three Men In A Boat, Jerome K. Jerome, Penguin (1970)

The Scoop by **James Plunkett** is taken from his *Collected Short Stories* (Poolbeg Press). Students may also enjoy his novel *Strumpet City* (Arrow Books).

Related reading:

Under Goliath, Peter Carter, Puffin (1980)
Across The Barricades, Joan Lingard, Puffin (1975)
Into Exile, Joan Lingard, Puffin (1974)
The Pedlar's Revenge and other stories, Liam O'Flaherty, Wolfhound Press (1982)
The Penguin Complete Saki, Penguin (1982)
Vintage Thurber (Volumes 1 and 2), Penguin (1983)
Humour, F. E. S. Finn (ed.), John Murray (1978)
A Game of Soldiers, Jan Needle, Fontana (1985)

Acknowledgements

The editor and publishers wish to thank the following for permission to reprint the short stories:

Virago Press Limited for 'To Da-duh, In Memoriam' from *Merle and Other Stories* by Paule Marshall, published by Virago Press Limited, 1985. Copyright © 1983 by Paule Marshall.

A. P. Watt Ltd Literary Agents for 'Chemistry' and 'The Tunnel' by Graham Swift from *Learning to Swim and Other Stories*, Picador, 1985. © Graham Swift, 1982.

Personal essay © Graham Swift, 1986.

Richard Scott Simon Ltd for 'The Custodian' by Susan Hill from the collection *A Bit of Singing and Dancing*, Hamish Hamilton Publishers, 1973. © Susan Hill, 1972.

Beverley Naidoo for 'The Gun' (previously unpublished). © Beverley Naidoo, 1986.

Personal essay © Beverley Naidoo, 1986.

Jessie Taylor for 'Lunch Hour Rush' by Roger Mais.

Longman Paul Limited, New Zealand for 'An Affair of the Heart' by Frank Sargeson from *The Stories of Frank Sargeson*, Penguin Books, 1982.

Sheba Feminist Publishers for 'Memento Mori' by Moy McCrory from the collection *The Water's Edge*, Sheba Feminist Publishers, 1985.

A. D. Peters & Co Ltd Writers' Agents for 'The Scoop' by James Plunkett from the collection *The Trusting and the Maimed*, Hutchinson Publishing Group Ltd, 1977.